"You Know You Want Me," He Said.

"You want me as much as I want you. It's been that way since that first time I kissed you."

"This is crazy."

"I'll go crazy if I can't have you."

Fire raged in his dark, compelling eyes; only, something else was there, as well—a challenge. He was challenging her to deny what he'd said on both counts. She couldn't, and he knew it.

Besides, he was right. To have sex with him was what she'd wanted, too; only, she hadn't even realized that until now, until he'd voiced that challenge.

Her gaze dropped. When at last she raised her head, her breathing was coming in short spurts.

"Ready to do something about it?"

"Garth—"

"Come here," he said, his voice raspy, almost unrecognizable.

Dear Reader,

I know you've all been anxiously awaiting the next book from Mary Lynn Baxter—so wait no more. Here it is, the MAN OF THE MONTH, *Tight-Fittin' Jeans*. Mary Lynn's books are known for their sexy heroes and sizzling sensuality...and this sure has both! Read and enjoy.

Every little girl dreams of marrying a handsome prince, but most women get to kiss a lot of toads before they find him. Read how three handsome princes find their very own princesses in Leanne Banks's delightful new miniseries HOW TO CATCH A PRINCESS. The fun begins this month with *The Five-Minute Bride*.

The other books this month are all so wonderful...you won't want to miss any of them! If you like humor, don't miss Maureen Child's *Have Bride, Need Groom*. For blazing drama, there's Sara Orwig's *A Baby for Mommy*. Susan Crosby's *Wedding Fever* provides a touch of dashing suspense. And Judith McWilliams's *Practice Husband* is warmly emotional.

There is something for everyone here at Desire! I hope you enjoy each and every one of these love stories.

Lucia Macro

Senior Editor

Please address questions and book requests to:
Silhouette Reader Service
U.S.: 3010 Walden Ave., P.O. Box 1325, Buffalo, NY 14269
Canadian: P.O. Box 609, Fort Erie, Ont. L2A 5X3

MARY LYNN BAXTER

TIGHT-FITTIN' JEANS

SILHOUETTE *Desire*

TM
Published by Silhouette Books

America's Publisher of Contemporary Romance

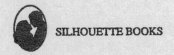

SILHOUETTE BOOKS

ISBN 0-373-76057-4

TIGHT-FITTIN' JEANS

Copyright © 1997 by Mary Lynn Baxter

Books by Mary Lynn Baxter

Silhouette Desire

Shared Moments #24
Added Delight #527
Winter Heat #542
Slow Burn #571
Tall in the Saddle #660
Marriage, Diamond Style #679
And Baby Makes Perfect #727
Mike's Baby #781
Dancler's Woman #822
Saddle Up #991
Tight-Fittin' Jeans #1057

Silhouette Special Edition

All Our Tomorrows #9
Tears of Yesterday #31
Autumn Awakening #96
Between the Raindrops #360

Silhouette Intimate Moments

Another Kind of Love #19
Memories that Linger #52
Everything But Time #74
A Handful of Heaven #117
Price Above Rubies #130
When We Touch #156
Fool's Music #197
Moonbeams Aplenty #217
Knight Sparks #272
Wish Giver #296

Silhouette Books

Silhouette Christmas Stories 1992
"Joni's Magic"

MARY LYNN BAXTER

sold hundreds of romances before she ever wrote one. The D&B Bookstore, right on the main drag in Lufkin, Texas, is her home as well as the store she owns and manages. She and her husband, Leonard, garden in their spare time. Around five o'clock every evening they can be found picking butter beans on their small farm just outside of town.

Prologue

Would today be the day he had another heart attack? Could be, Garth Dixon told himself, especially when he felt as if a hippo were sitting on his chest. What bothered him the most was wondering when the "big one" was going to hit. He'd already come face-to-face with his mortality, and he hadn't been impressed, since he was only forty.

Realizing he was using the rickety post on the porch to hold himself upright, he straightened to his full six-foot-two-inch height. Hell, the doctors might think he had one foot in the coffin and the other on a banana peel, but he was determined to prove them wrong.

His ticker would be good as new if he could just survive this godforsaken place. Ah, Pennington, Utah. If anyone had told him he would end up in this small farming and ranching community, holed up in a rustic cabin, nursing a cantankerous heart, he would have laughed.

Well, he wasn't laughing now, not by a long shot. He wasn't sure he would be able to laugh again until he was away from here and back in Dallas, in his corporate offices. Just thinking about that, and all the work he'd been forced to leave behind, caused a tight squeezing around his chest, something he couldn't allow to happen.

The problem was, he didn't have anything else to think about. Work was his life. The only thing in front of him now was the sun setting in the west, perhaps the most beautiful sunset he'd ever seen. But then, he wasn't into sunsets. If that was all he had to look forward to, then he might as well sit on a keg of dynamite and wait for it to blow.

He needed a challenge. He needed something he could sink his teeth into, which was exactly what he could *not* do. So what did that leave? Learning to be a connoisseur of sunsets? God forbid.

Yet, like it or not, he had to alter his life-style, or else. It was the ''or else'' that made the sweat suddenly pop out on his skin as if he were a teenager at his first dance. He would do what he had to do; he always had. He'd had to learn to live with the scars on his soul, but it would be a cold day in hell before he lived with them on his heart.

Disgusted with his thoughts, Garth glared at the sunset once more, with reinforced resentment, then tromped back inside the cabin. He was about to plop down on the couch when the phone rang. He stopped in midaction. This was the first time in a week he'd heard that sound.

Garth grimaced, thinking that before he'd been forced into this change of scenery, he'd come to think of the receiver as a permanent part of his body. He wished it was his office calling, but he knew that wouldn't be the case. Under no circumstances were they to bother him. His family, however, was a different matter.

"Dixon," he said, then realized he didn't recognize the voice on the other end of the line.

Once the conversation had ended, Garth hung up, a bit disconcerted. The caller was a man who owned a nearby ranch, Jeremiah Davis, whom he had run into on several occasions at Irma Quill's general store.

Garth paused in his thoughts, a smile relaxing his drawn features as his mind switched gears to Irma, who was in a class all her own. In fact, he'd never met anyone like her, except in books and on TV. With her birdlike features and antiquated way of dressing, bonnet and all, she reminded him of a character straight out of "Little House on the Prairie."

Since he'd been in Pennington, Irma seemed to have taken a liking to him, though he hadn't encouraged her. Still, when she insisted on loading him down with home-made bread and jam, he hadn't turned it down; the smell never failed to revive his appetite.

However, it wasn't Irma he should be thinking about now, but rather, the favor Jeremiah Davis had asked of him. Jeremiah had told him there had been an emergency in his family and asked Garth if he would keep an eye on things while he was away, explaining that he was leaving his daughter behind with a friend.

Garth had consented, though he wasn't excited about the neighborly deed, as he didn't particularly want to be neighborly.

Hell, all he wanted was a one-way ticket back to Texas.

One

"**Y**ou don't run this department, you know."

Tiffany Russell eyed her boss, at the same time swallowing a scathing retort. She was well aware that she wasn't in charge of ladies' fine apparel, and that was the problem. She knew she *should* be.

Hazel Mason, unaffectionately known as "Witch Hazel," might have enough style to make her large, rawboned stature seem elegant, rather than offensive, but that was as far as her assets went. Tiffany held fast to the notion that the woman's tongue was sharper than her mind. When it came to doing something different, to branching out, Hazel was not interested, period.

Tiffany mellowed her voice as much as she could. "I'm aware of that, Hazel. Still, I can't see why you object to entering the twentieth century."

"If that's meant to be funny, it isn't."

"Look," Tiffany said, pushing a wad of natural blond

hair behind her ear, "if we don't do something soon, the competition is going to continue to kick our butt right into oblivion."

"And you seriously think your idea of half-naked models parading through the racks serving pineapple is going to up the sales?"

"I do."

"Well, I don't." Hazel's tone was as cold as her blue eyes. "Even if I agreed with the beach-party idea, which I don't, that line of swimwear you want to buy is simply too far-out for our ladies."

"I beg to differ with you," Tiffany countered, standing firm. "Anyway, how will we know until we try?"

"It's simply too costly a gamble. And since I have the final word, it's not going to happen."

Tiffany literally had to bite her lip to keep from voicing another opinion, one that would most likely get her fired, even though keeping her thoughts to herself went against her grain. She wanted to lash out at this woman, whose face now reminded her of a prune, it was so severely wrinkled in distaste.

She doubted Hazel's hair had ever been out of that bun, or that she'd ever done anything daring, such as wearing a two-piece bathing suit. The idea of her parading naked in front of a man was even more incredible. How she'd ever had two kids was beyond Tiffany. She would bet her favorite Magic Lift Bra that Hazel and her husband made love with the lights out and the covers over their heads.

"Well?"

Tiffany shook her head and stared at her boss. "Well, what?"

"Don't you have work to do?"

"Right."

A few minutes later, Tiffany was back in the stock-room, staring at the boxes of clothing that had arrived late yesterday afternoon. Ordinarily, she would have torn open the boxes filled with lovely clothes and accessories with vigorous anticipation, thinking of how lucky she was to have Christmas on a daily basis.

But not today. She was still seething from her go-round with Witch Hazel. These confrontations were coming far too often. Tiffany loved her work, though she didn't necessarily love the company she worked for. As a buyer for women's clothing for Cunningham's at the Galleria, she had her own ideas of the market and what would sell and what would not.

Unfortunately, her boss did not agree with her.

Feeling her frustration and anger rising, Tiffany turned her back on the boxes and made her way into her office, which was nothing but a cubbyhole. But it was hers, and she could be alone there and give in to the emotions churning inside her.

She perched on the edge of her desk and swung her foot. Hell's bells, maybe she ought to quit. But she wasn't a quitter. Too, she wasn't ready to give Hazel the satisfaction of running her off. She couldn't deny, though, that she was going home every day with a head-ache.

Suddenly Tiffany's frown burgeoned into a smile as thoughts of her best friend, Bridget, leaped to mind. At one time, Bridget's career as an attorney had been in the toilet, or so she had thought. Now she was happily married and living in a small town in Utah.

Tiffany's smile broadened. She took full responsibility for her friend's sudden and unorthodox marriage. Why, if she hadn't insisted Bridget attend that crazy bachelor auction, she wouldn't have bid on Jeremiah Davis and won him.

Tiffany laughed out loud as she thought back on the moment when Bridget had lunged out of her chair and yelled, "One thousand dollars!"

Aghast, Tiffany had jerked Bridget back down in her seat. However, the damage had already been done. Bridget had gotten what she paid for, a tall, slow-talking rancher who wasn't about to let the best thing that had ever happened to him slip through his fingers.

Shaking her head, Tiffany eased off the desk and walked over to where she kept her two-cup coffeemaker. She filled a cup full of French vanilla and sipped; although it soothed her stomach, it did nothing for her clicking mind.

While she envied Bridget many things, her marriage was not one of them. Tiffany had come close to getting married only once; thank God it hadn't come about. The man had been—and still was—a lush, though she hadn't realized it. Even at thirty, which years ago would have classified her as an old maid, a ring on her finger wasn't what she wanted. Her desires leaned more toward life's amenities: a great job, a nice house, a fancy car and a hefty bank account, and not necessarily in that order, either.

Although she had none of the above at the moment, Tiffany intended to remedy that. Her goal was to eventually have enough money, borrowed or otherwise, to open her own shop, a shop that catered to rich and privileged women. Working at Cunningham's was merely a stepping-stone.

Tiffany took another generous mouthful of coffee, savoring the taste, only to have it tainted by sudden thoughts of Hazel. She wasn't sure just how much longer she could take the woman's abuse, along with her lack of enthusiasm. She had about as much innovative energy as molasses running uphill.

"Grrr," Tiffany muttered, then drained her cup.

There had to be a way to get through to her boss without jeopardizing her job. At the moment, however, nothing came to mind. She was always walking that fine line between getting ahead and getting canned.

Another smile flirted with her lips as thoughts of Bridget resurfaced. It had been only a little over a year since she and Bridget had had that conversation about how low both their lives had sunk.

Of course, Bridget's hadn't, not really, since she was from a wealthy family here in Houston, with money of her own, to boot. Tiffany, on the other hand, had nothing to fall back on—no family and no money.

That was why she couldn't waltz into Hazel's office and tell her what she could do with her antiquated ideas and this job.

"Yo."

Tiffany, unaware that her privacy had been invaded, jumped, then whipped around. The intruder was Gretchen Wheeler, one of the salesclerks.

"Sorry," Gretchen said. "Didn't mean to scare you."

"You didn't. What's up?"

Gretchen made a face. "Hazel's dander."

"Great."

"She wants to see you."

"What else is new?" Tiffany's mouth curved downward. "I get out of her sight for five minutes and she goes berserk."

Gretchen gave her a sympathetic look, though she appeared uncomfortable at being the go-between who bore the unhappy message.

"Thanks," Tiffany finally said, letting Gretchen off the hook. "I'll see you later."

Gretchen nodded, then left. Tiffany stood for a moment, contemplating walking into Hazel's office and telling her what she could do with both her demands and the job; then the phone rang.

Thinking it was the witch adding insult to injury, Tiffany grabbed the receiver and said a curt "Yes."

"Whoa! Down, girl."

Tiffany threw back her head and laughed, having recognized the voice right off. "Why, Jeremiah Davis, fancy you calling me." Then her voice sobered and her stomach lurched, as it dawned on her that something was amiss. First off, Jeremiah was calling, instead of Bridget, and second, it was in the middle of the day. "I take it this isn't a social call."

"You're right."

Her stomach gave another lurch, and at the same time fear clogged her throat; she couldn't utter a word. Something must have happened to Bridget or Jeremiah's six-year-old daughter, Taylor, from his first marriage.

As if Jeremiah had picked up on her fear, he went on, "It's Bridget. She's been injured in a car accident, but she's going to be okay."

Tiffany picked up on the desperate ring to his voice, but she didn't acknowledge it. "Thank God," she whispered, sitting down before her knees could give way under her. "Was she alone?"

"Yeah. She slammed into a school bus, which caused damage to her spine and legs."

"How much damage?" Tiffany hated asking that question, but she had no choice. She might as well know the good, the bad and the ugly now as later.

"She's partially paralyzed, though the doctor says it's not permanent."

"What can I do to help?"

Jeremiah hemmed and hawed, then finally said, "I was wondering if it's possible for you to take some vacation time and baby-sit Taylor. I can't leave Bridget, and my aunt's not able to keep Taylor. She's had a slight stroke, and..." He hesitated. "I wouldn't ask, but—"

"I'd be insulted if you hadn't." And Tiffany meant it, even though she didn't have any vacation time left. Maybe all wasn't lost. Maybe this unexpected twist of events was the answer to her problem.

She could resign, then look for another job when she returned from Utah. Although her savings account was far from what she wanted it to be, it wasn't all that shabby. If she had to, she could dip into that, then replace what she'd used.

"Tiffany?"

"I'm on my way."

With that, she replaced the receiver, then listened as her heart banged against her rib cage. Even though she was concerned for her friend, she suddenly felt like a prisoner who had just been released from death row.

"Yes, yes, yes!"

She left her office and headed straight for Hazel's, a bounce in her steps.

Two

Tiffany stood in the small hospital room in Hurricane, where Bridget had been taken following the accident, though Tiffany had yet to talk to her. A lab tech was in the process of drawing blood from Bridget's arm.

Unable to watch the procedure, Tiffany kept her eyes averted. Needles gave her the willies, especially when they were used to penetrate the skin.

She had contemplated going to the ranch first and dumping her bags. But in her eagerness to see for herself that her friend was *not* critical, she had rented a car at the airport and come straight here.

Jeremiah had insisted on meeting her flight, but she'd insisted otherwise, pointing out that he needn't be concerned about her, that he had enough on his plate at the moment. As if he'd realized she was as headstrong as his wife, he'd let out a sigh and given in.

Now, as Tiffany continued to wait, she peered out the

window into a park, serene and breathtakingly lovely with cottonwood, pecan and mulberry trees galore. She had forgotten just how beautiful this part of the country was, even in July. When she stepped outside at the airport, she had felt the incredible heat, but it wasn't that humid, cloying heat that was so much a part of southeast Texas.

Yet she wouldn't trade Texas for Utah, not in this lifetime, anyway. She had to smile, still unable to comprehend how her socialite friend, Bridget, had managed to adapt so well. Tiffany sighed out loud. She guessed love had brought about that miracle.

Thank God she was immune from that bug biting her, especially if it meant she had to remain in these parts. Tiffany made a face. Oh, Hurricane, which was a fairly nice-size town, was all right. In fact, compared to Pennington, where Bridget and Jeremiah lived, it was a thriving metropolis. Still, there was nothing in either place for her except her dear friend.

Living in the woods, off the land, was not for her. As soon as she had fulfilled her loving obligation, she would be gone, back to the bright lights.

"Tiff, you made it."

At the sound of Bridget's voice, Tiffany swung around. She didn't move, though, until the nurse and lab tech had left. Then she made her way toward the bed. But at the sight of her friend's pinched features, Tiffany's forthcoming smile didn't materialize. Under close scrutiny, Bridget seemed a mere shadow of her former self.

Tiffany hadn't seen Bridget since she married Jeremiah, which was a year ago now. Bridget's short red hair had been vibrant, and her brown eyes had been alive with fire and humor. Both had diminished to a shocking degree.

A chill darted through Tiffany. Had Jeremiah glossed over the situation? Was Bridget's condition much worse than he'd let on? Tiffany knew that he loved his wife more than life itself and couldn't contemplate the thought of her being less than whole. Perhaps that thought alone accounted for his inability to face facts.

Tiffany, forcing a smile, stepped closer to the bed. Despite Bridget's obvious attempt to reciprocate the smile, her mouth was pinched with pain.

"Hi, sweetie," Tiffany said, leaning closer and brushing Bridget's warm cheek with her lips.

Bridget grabbed her friend's hand, tears filling her eyes. "I'm so glad you're here. I was afraid you couldn't come. Or wouldn't."

"Hogwash," Tiffany responded in a low voice, all the while fighting back her own tears. If she gave in and boo-hooed the way she wanted to, the room would wash away. Besides, now was not the time to let her emotions have free rein. She had to maintain a brave front, for Bridget's sake. "Nothing short of two broken legs would've kept me away."

"I can believe that. When you make up your mind, you're the stubbornest, most hardheaded person I know."

"All I can say is, it takes one to know one."

They both chuckled, then fell silent.

Tiffany was the first to break that silence. "So, where do you go from here?"

"To a specialty hospital in Vegas, where they're going to put me in traction for heaven only knows how long—several weeks, I imagine."

"Stretch the old bod, huh? Ouch!"

"I know," Bridget said in a wan tone. "I can't tell you how badly I dread it, but I have to get well, and not just for myself, either. There's Jeremiah and Taylor."

Tiffany heard the desperation in her friend's voice, and it broke her heart. "Shh...don't work yourself up into a dither. You're going to be just fine. And you do want to get well for yourself. Why, you know you're irreplaceable on the end of that hoe. From what I understand, you've developed magic in them there fingers."

Bridget rolled her eyes. "Yeah, right. It would be closer to the truth to say that Jeremiah tolerates my crooked rows and merely turns his head when I mistake plants for weeds and chop them down."

"Oh, well," Tiffany said with a grin, "I bet he prefers your other talents to that one, such as your ability to cook a mean Lean Cuisine."

"If I live to be an old lady leaning on a cane, I'll never live that one down."

"You sure won't."

"So, how long can you stay?" Bridget asked.

"As long as I'm needed."

"Thank God. I hate leaving Taylor. She's upset, and—"

"Hey, she's going to be just fine. Aunt Tiffany's going to see to that. We'll be big buddies before you know it. All you have to do is get well."

"I feel like such an idiot. If I'd been concentrating on my driving instead of the carnival at Taylor's play school, then I wouldn't have had the accident."

"What exactly happened? I haven't had a chance to talk to Jeremiah about the details."

"I was blinded by the sun, and before I knew it, I was looking at the rear of a school bus. In order not to hit it, I veered, then lost control. The next thing I knew I was skidding down an embankment, straight for a tree.''

"God, you're lucky it didn't mangle your insides."

"I credit my seat belt with saving my life." Bridget paused. "Still, I have a long way to go before I'll be one hundred percent." Her voice broke. "I was hoping to get pregnant, and now that's out of the question."

"For now, but not forever. Just remember that. Besides, you're like me. You're a fighter. In a few months, your curvy bod will be as good as new."

"Oh, Tiff, you're so good *to* me, and *for* me." Bridget's voice cracked again. "I'm so thankful you came, and so is Jeremiah. It's been terribly hard on him, with the ranch and all."

"The ranch has nothing to do with it. He's certifiable because he's so damn crazy in love with you."

"I feel the same way about him." Bridget brushed back a tear. "I know why both he and Taylor are so upset. After all, Jeremiah's already lost one wife, and Taylor lost her mother."

"Well, they are *not* going to lose you."

"They nearly did."

"Well, nearly ain't the real thing." Tiffany grinned, then changed the subject. "I never thought your marriage would last, you know."

"No one did, least of all my parents."

"Well, getting drunk, then, a few hours later, marrying a man you won in an auction, does lead one toward skepticism."

"It was fate at its best." Bridget shrugged. "What more can I say?"

"I'd say that pretty well sums it up."

"So what about you? I didn't by any chance pull you out of the clutches of any man?"

"Not no, but *hell* no!"

"Tiff!"

"Don't 'Tiff' me. I'm not interested in ties that bind. I'm only interested in jump-starting my career and making money."

"So what did this trip do to those plans?"

Tiffany laughed. "It brought relief from the boss from hell."

"Not as in, you were fired, I hope."

"I quit, actually."

"Oh, Tiff, I feel awful."

"Don't. I've been aching to do it for months. That call from Jeremiah was just the push I needed."

Bridget laughed. "I can just see you marching into her office."

"That's exactly what I did." Tiffany grinned. "I would have given anything if you could've been a fly on the wall and seen the look on Witch Hazel's face when I told her in a nice way to kiss my you-know-what, that I was outa there."

"I just hope you didn't make a mistake."

"No way." Tiffany's grin strengthened. "I don't anticipate ever being in that position again."

"You lovable idiot."

"That's me," Tiffany quipped, peering at her watch. "Look, I'd better get going. I'm surprised a nurse hasn't been in and run me off."

"As badly as I hate to see you go, Taylor'll be in from play school soon, and I'd like for you to be there."

Tiffany leaned over again and kissed her friend on the cheek. "You hang in there, okay? Everything's going to be just fine."

Later, as Tiffany walked out into the bright sunlight, she paused and took several deep breaths. Bridget had to be all right. She just *had* to.

"Hey, squirt, what've you been doing? Making mud pies in your ears?"

Taylor giggled, then gazed up at Tiffany. "You're being silly."

"I'm being truthful, young lady. I don't think you've had that washcloth anywhere near that part of your body."

Taylor giggled again, but she made no effort to shift the rag to her head, which Tiffany saw as her first challenge with this precocious six-year-old.

In fact, all the way to the ranch from the hospital, apprehension had gnawed at her. What if she'd bitten off more than she could chew? Hell, what she knew about children could fill a thimble. But since she had no choice, she had to make the best of the situation, no matter what.

Jeremiah and Taylor had both come out to the car to meet her. The first time she had seen the child, with her doelike brown eyes and long, shiny hair, Tiffany had fallen under her spell. Taylor seemed to have bonded with her as well.

Now, two days later, with Jeremiah and Bridget at the hospital in Las Vegas, that love affair was threatened, and all because of mud pies in the ears.

"I couldn't find Piper Girl," Taylor was saying.

Tiffany shook her head. "What did you say?"

The child repeated her statement.

"Who is Piper Girl?"

"My kitty."

"Ah, I see."

"She sleeps on the foot of my bed."

Great. Tiffany hated cats, but she would bite her tongue before admitting that. "So, I wonder where Piper Girl is?"

"In the barn, eating a rat."

"Swell."

"Would you go get her and bring her inside?"

"Only if you promise she won't eat me."

Taylor threw her a look. "She doesn't even bite. She's a sweetie."

That remained to be seen, Tiffany told herself, then said out loud, "I'll make you a deal. I'll get the kitty if you'll let me get rid of the mud pies."

"Oh, all right," Taylor said, handing Tiffany the cloth.

A few minutes later, a powdered-down Taylor was in her bedroom, putting on her pajamas. Tiffany watched her for a minute, then said, "I'll be right back, hopefully with kitty in tow."

Garth Dixon tightened the girth, then climbed into the saddle. Although the horse snorted and nodded its head indicating it was ready to go, Garth didn't nudge the animal into action. He simply sat there lost in thought. He didn't want to do this chore. He didn't want to do anything that required an effort, and being neighborly certainly required that.

As it was, he'd put off doing the favor Jeremiah Davis had asked of him to the point that he couldn't indulge himself any longer. That didn't mean he had to like it.

But again, if he was going to live in this place, he should work on his attitude, which meant he shouldn't mind helping someone out, especially a man whose desperation had been clear even on the phone. Garth guessed he would feel the same way if his wife was laid up in the hospital seriously injured.

Well, on second thought... A jerk of his head veered him off the track. Just do the good deed and get it over with, he told himself. It was such a small thing and here he was making a big deal out of it, which was par for the course. These days even getting out of bed was a big deal, not to mention his poor attitude, something he refused to apologize for.

Sighing, Garth finally nudged the horse and moved in sync with its big but graceful body, the pace leisurely as he guided his mount through the wooded, fertile valley toward the Davis ranch.

Though he continued to nurse his sour mood, he couldn't ignore the beauty and peace that surrounded him. Still, it wasn't peace he sought. He'd already had enough of that to last him a lifetime.

A short time later, Garth ambled onto the Davis property. Having decided to check the barn before heading toward the house, he dismounted and went inside.

After looking around and finding nothing amiss, he breathed a sigh of relief. Once he checked the house, he could get back to his cabin in the woods.

He smiled a bitter smile.

Tiffany was halfway to the barn when she stopped for a moment, noticing, not for the first time, how liberating it felt to be here and away from the evils of her former job. She stared into the distance, taking in the beauty of the fertile valley, including the surrounding rolling hills and distant mountains. Maybe this was the panacea she had needed to get her life back on track, though she would give anything to have been here under different circumstances.

Refusing to dwell on the negative, Tiffany made her way into the barn, ruing the deal she'd made with Taylor. With nightfall fast approaching, the barn gave her the creeps, not to mention having to cart that cat back to the house.

She was about to call out "kitty, kitty" when she saw him. Tiffany's footsteps faltered at the same time that her heart jumped into her throat. Her initial reaction to seeing a strange man on the premises was to run, to get the hell out of Dodge.

Instead, while his back was to her, she acted on impulse and latched on to the garden shovel that, luckily, was at her fingertips. Then she raised her weapon and brought it down on his skull.

She didn't know which emotion was more exhilarating—horror or relief—as he dropped to his knees, then fell facedown in the dirt.

Three

Tiffany stared wild-eyed at the hunk of humanity sprawled in front of her. Who was he? And what was he doing on the Davis property? Was he homeless, perhaps looking for a place to sleep? Even though she couldn't tell much about him, the latter somehow didn't ring true. From what she could see of him, he wasn't dressed like a vagrant. He had on a pair of okay-looking jeans, a casual shirt and boots.

He was tall and thin, too thin to suit her taste. That aside, he could have passed for any Texas cowboy on any given day—only this cowboy wasn't moving.

Making tiny mewing sounds against the hand she was holding across her mouth, Tiffany backed up, never taking her eyes off him. What had she done? *Had she killed him?*

OhmyGodohmyGod, she chanted silently, until she backed into the door frame. Then, on legs that seemed to have a will of their own, she turned and tore off toward the house. By the time she reached the back porch, she was so weak and sick to her stomach that she had to catch a post and hold on to it, reaching deep inside herself for a decent breath.

Dear Lord, she didn't want to spend the rest of her life behind bars, which might be what would happen if she'd actually hit him hard enough to kill him. And she was very much afraid that she had. She'd seen the blood trickling down the side of his head. Her stomach did another flip-flop, and it was all she could do not to give in to the desire to lean over and throw up.

But she couldn't allow herself that luxury. Regardless of who he was—rapist, thief, or vagrant—she had to get help. As it was, she'd wasted enough time. She crossed to the door and flung it open.

Taylor was sitting on the couch with the TV blaring, laughing at the show she was watching. When she saw Tiffany, she seemed to sense that something was wrong.

"Are you sick?" she asked with childlike bluntness.

Tiffany threw her what she hoped was a reassuring smile, but she knew she'd failed. Taylor looked almost as terrified as she felt herself.

"I have to call 911."

"We don't have 911."

"Damn," Tiffany muttered. Of course this one-horse community wouldn't have such a sophisticated system.

"That's a naughty word. My mommy said you're not supposed to say it."

"What?"

"Damn."

If the situation hadn't been so serious, Tiffany would have laughed. But the situation *was* serious, and now was not the time to deal with the issue of whether she'd said something she shouldn't have.

"Forget I said that, okay?"

"Okay."

"I'll have to call the sheriff," Tiffany said, more to herself than for Taylor's benefit. Noticing that the number she sought was posted by the phone, she snatched up the receiver and dialed.

Moments later, the terse conversation was behind her, but still she couldn't seem to move or to think rationally. Only after Taylor jumped off the couch and stared at her as if she had just landed from another planet did she react.

She'd said as little as possible, so as not to frighten the child more than she had to. "It's going to be all right," Tiffany said now, in what she prayed was a calm and rational tone.

Taylor's lower lip trembled. "I want my daddy and mommy."

"So do I, kiddo, but unfortunately, you're stuck with me."

Tears flooded the child's eyes, and Tiffany felt like an inept idiot. She placed her arms around Taylor's shoulders and held her close.

She couldn't believe this was happening. Had she actually whacked another human over the head so hard that she might have taken his life?

No! Now that she was safely in the house, away from the eerie barn, she wouldn't think like that. Surely she hadn't done that much damage to his head. She didn't have that much strength. Or did she? Maybe she'd cracked him in just the right place. Again the sick feeling washed over her, and she saw herself being handcuffed, then put in the sheriff's car.

Tiffany swallowed the panic that rose up the back of her throat just as she heard the siren.

Taylor twisted out of her arms and rushed to the window. "Sheriff Wright's getting out of the car."

Tiffany didn't wait for him to knock. She headed for the door herself, Taylor on her heels. "Uh-uh, young lady. You stay put right here."

Taylor's face bunched into a frown. "I don't want to."

"Nevertheless, you're going to." Then, softening her words, Tiffany added, "As soon as I know what's going on, I'll be back."

Taylor jutted her chin and averted her face. Tiffany hated knowing that the child was upset, but there wasn't anything she could do about that at the moment. There was enough trauma going on in Taylor's life without her seeing a man who might be—

Shutting down that thought, Tiffany raced out the door just as the sheriff walked onto the porch. "Howdy, ma'am," he said, tipping his hat. "I'm Porter Wright."

It wasn't that he was tall and lean to the point of gauntness, or that he wore a Fu Manchu mustache, that made her wince inwardly, but rather the smell that surrounded him—as if he'd just stepped in a patty of cow manure.

Unwittingly, she lowered her head, and sure enough, he had. His boots were caked with it. This time it was all Tiffany could do to hold her already queasy stomach in check.

"I'm Tiffany Russell," she said at last.

"Suppose you take me to where this fellow is."

"He's...he's in the barn."

"Let's go have a look-see."

"Do I have to go with you?"

The sheriff removed his hat and scratched his head. "I don't suppose so."

"Never mind, I'll come. I have to face the music sooner or later."

Porter Wright gave her a strange look before commenting, "Most likely you're in the clear, whoever this person is. Folks around here get real nervous when someone invades their privacy. You did the right thing, I'm sure."

"Taylor, honey, I'll be right back," Tiffany called into the house. "You'll be fine."

Although it had been only fifteen minutes since the incident, it seemed like an eternity as Tiffany followed Sheriff Wright back to the barn.

He entered first. Tiffany pulled up short behind him, just inside the door, and clung to the rustic facing for dear life, despite the fact that splinters were digging into her hand.

The man was sitting up and in the process of wiping the blood off his temple. Relief left her feeling even weaker than the earlier bouts of nausea. She opened her mouth to speak, but nothing came out. All she could do was stand there gaping at him, all the while praising the Lord that he was alive and she wouldn't be going to the penitentiary.

The man, however, wasn't at a loss for words. In fact, the expletives spilling from his lips sent the color rushing back into Tiffany's face. She felt as if she'd suddenly caught a fever.

"Should I...call an ambulance?" she stammered.

"Hell, no!"

"Well, I'll be damned," Sheriff Wright said, his features wrinkled in a grin.

"I'm glad you think it's funny," the man snapped,

rising fully to his feet, though he was obviously still unsteady, and glaring at the sheriff.

Tiffany felt the urge to race to him and help him, but she knew that wouldn't be the thing to do. He looked mad enough to chew a barbed-wire fence in two.

"Ms. Tiffany Russell, meet the man you've just waylaid," Wright said. "Jeremiah's neighbor, Garth Dixon."

"Oh, no," Tiffany whispered, but the words were loud enough for both men to hear.

"Oh, yes, Ms. Russell, or whoever the hell you are," Garth lashed back.

Tiffany took a step forward, a hand outstretched. "Look, Mr. Dixon, I'm sorry. I didn't mean—"

He cursed again, cutting her off in midsentence. "Like hell you didn't mean it. You nearly took my damn head off with that shovel."

Tiffany flung a helpless look at Porter Wright. The sheriff seemed content to stand back and let the two of them go at it, grinning all the while, as if he were enjoying the exchange to the max.

Well, why not? Tiffany thought. This incident was probably the most exciting thing that had happened around these parts in a long time. She would have liked nothing better than to knock that grin off Wright's face, then turn around and knock the smirk off Dixon's. Instead, she swallowed her own mounting anger and said, "If only you'd come to the house and told me who you were, I wouldn't—"

"Hell, lady, that doesn't excuse you, especially since I wasn't a threat to you."

"How was I to know that?"

Garth Dixon looked at her as if he wanted to throttle

her, which she was sure he did, in retaliation for what she'd done to him.

"Hell, I see I'm wasting my time talking to you. Anyone that dizzy—"

Tiffany was enraged. "I'll have you know that I'm not—"

"Save it, lady. I'm not interested."

Instead of barking right back at him the way she wanted to do, Tiffany turned and stomped toward the door. Once there, she had second thoughts, and she whirled around, glaring at him. Who did he think he was? She wouldn't let him get away with placing all the blame on her shoulders.

She was about to voice that thought when her gut instinct kicked in, telling her that for now she'd best keep her mouth shut, if she wanted to come out the winner here. For one thing, the man was in obvious pain. But more than that, he was livid, livid to the point that she knew her impulsiveness had gained her an enemy, which was too bad.

Garth Dixon was a good-looking man, even if he was a bit too thin. Pure eye candy. Even the red, purplish lump on the side of his head didn't detract from the dramatics of his chiseled features, his salt-and-pepper hair—more salt than pepper—or the dark blue eyes surrounded by thick black lashes.

Too bad again that she didn't give a fig if he was handsome or not. Not only was he too old for her—she guessed him to be in his forties—he was a poor sodbuster, which was an even bigger turnoff than his age.

Her grandmother had always told her that she could fall in love with a rich man as easily as a poor one. Tiffany had never forgotten those pearls of wisdom. But then, she didn't have to worry. She wasn't about to fall in love with any man, certainly not this one, who continued to look at her through cold, hostile eyes.

"Surely you were aware that Jeremiah asked me to keep an eye on the place while he was gone?" Garth asked at last.

"No, I wasn't."

"Well, hell."

"If it's an apology you want," Tiffany said, "then you've got it."

Sheriff Wright shoved himself away from the post where he'd been leaning. "I guess that settles things, then. If Ms. Russell here is willing to apologize, then—"

"I don't want her apology." Garth focused his fierce gaze on Tiffany, then spoke directly to her. "All I want is for you to stay the hell away from me."

With that, he turned and, cutting around her, stalked out of the barn.

"Whew!" Sheriff Wright said, taking off his hat and fanning his face. "I'd say he's madder than a stirred-up hornet's nest."

"He'll get over it," Tiffany countered, tight-lipped.

"I sure hope so, ma'am. For your sake, that is."

"What do you mean by that?"

"According to Irma Quill, he's been real sick, something about a bad heart."

Tiffany's own heart took a nosedive as another bout of guilt rose to the surface. "What else do you know about him?"

"Nothing, except he's apparently about as close-mouthed as they come, and he hasn't been in the community but a few months."

Tiffany held out her hand. "Thanks for coming, Sheriff. I appreciate it very much."

"Just doing my job, ma'am. Come on, I'll walk you

back to the house. I'm sure that young'n's having a conniption fit."

"You're right," Tiffany said, another pang of guilt
stabbing her.

A short time later, after explaining to the child what
had happened, though without the details, Tiffany sat on
the bed beside Taylor, tucking her in for the night.

"I'm so proud of you. You acted like such a big girl."

"I *am* a big girl. I'm six years old, going on seven."

"That's right, you are." Tiffany smiled, but the child
didn't. "What's the matter, honey?"

The child's gaze didn't waver. "I'm glad you found
my kitty, but my daddy's going to be real mad, 'cause
you hit his friend."

Four

___

Garth stumbled into the cabin and onto the couch. Sweat poured off his face like a broken water faucet. But the sweat was the least of his worries. His chest felt as if it were going to cave in on him at any second.

He shouldn't have pushed his horse at such a rapid clip through the woods. He'd been so pissed off over what had just happened that he'd let his temper overrule his sound judgment. Hell, he wasn't used to taking it easy. Since he could remember, he'd gotten up literally at the crack of dawn, taken a shower, then headed to the office, where he'd drunk a pot of coffee while planning which corporations to take over and which not to.

Now he couldn't do any of those things, except shower. And on some mornings even that was an effort. If his health and his mood didn't hurry up and change drastically, then he would just as soon bail out of this

life. Movers and shakers like himself weren't cut out to
be ill.

Garth leaned his head back on the couch and placed
his hand over his heart. Maybe he should go to the ER.
No, that was out. *Hospitals* were out. Besides, his heart
rate had settled, though not exactly back to normal. Not
only had anger at being in this situation and this godforsaken place sapped his precious energy, but embar-
rassment at having been banged on the head by that
dizzy blonde had added insult to injury.

"Damn!" he muttered, recalling the instant he'd
turned and seen her standing there, knowing beyond a
doubt that she was the one who had hit him. She'd had
that guilty look written all over her. For a moment he'd
fought the urge to grab her shoulders and shake her. But
since he'd never put his hands on a woman in that way,
the thought had died a natural death.

Still, Garth couldn't help but remember that even in
his dazed state, it hadn't been Tiffany Russell's face that
caught his attention, but rather the way her butt was
made for those tight-fittin' jeans she had on.

Then, as quickly as that thought had surfaced, it disappeared. He hadn't come here to get involved with a
woman. However, if the circumstances had been different, he would have asked her out, despite the fact that
he was sure her looks far outweighed her brainpower.
At this juncture in his life, that point didn't matter. He
was only interested in the pleasure, without the perma-
nency.

Yeah, she was a looker, all right, with shoulder-length
blond hair worn in a pageboy style, skin that reminded
him of rich cream and deep-set green eyes that appeared
so innocent. He almost choked on that thought.

Still, it was the way her well-endowed rear had filled

those jeans that seemed branded on his mind. Yet he couldn't overlook her voice; even though she had given an apology grudgingly, it had come out sounding like silk.

Unfortunately, the woman and her assets didn't mean a hill of beans to him. Another woman in his life was the last thing he needed or wanted. What he did want was to recover both in body and mind and return to his work a whole man.

Meanwhile, he was still breathing, which he had to think of as a gift and run with. If only he could let go of the notion that he had something to prove, not only to himself but to his stepfather, who had set him up in business. If only...

Determined not to open that can of worms, Garth stood. When the room stopped spinning, he trudged into the kitchen, where he poured himself a glass of orange juice. Frowning, he gulped it down, pretending it was Scotch on the rocks.

"Dream on, Dixon," he quipped, setting the empty glass on the cabinet. His days of drinking as much booze as he wanted were gone, along with so many of the other pleasures he had enjoyed. He vowed that that would only be temporary.

After his heart healed and he clinched the biggest business deal of his career, which was now on hold, then maybe he would give some thought to getting off that high-profile treadmill, even to semiretiring.

Sure thing, he told himself, knowing that was never going to happen. He wasn't like the majority of his buddies, who played golf as many hours a day as they could squeeze in and thought that was the ultimate challenge. He didn't go for that.

What he did go for was getting well, by far the biggest

challenge he'd ever faced. Garth's thoughts suddenly took him back to the time immediately after he'd been released from the hospital.

He'd headed straight for the sanctuary of his office, where he'd sat behind his desk, numb with shock and despair, his head in his hands.

He hadn't heard his right-hand man, Max Lansing, come in, until Max cleared his throat and said, "What the hell are you doing here? You should be home in bed."

Garth had stared at Max for a moment, taking in his stocky, muscled frame, his healthy, ruddy complexion, and felt green with envy. Then, feeling like a coward, he'd turned away.

Max had pressed him. "Well?"

"I couldn't go home. It's that simple."

"So what did the doctor say?"

"In a nutshell, if I don't slow down and take a few months' leave of absence, I won't live to see my fiftieth birthday."

"That's a crock of crap. I thought all this modern medical technology could fix anything."

Garth smirked. "Me too. But I want my ticker fixed as good as new, which apparently no one can do."

"So what's next?"

He didn't answer Max right off. He couldn't. The words were jammed in his throat. He coughed twice; only then could he speak. "I'm hauling ass." Bitterness underlined each word.

Max blinked. "Where to?"

"A remote part of Utah."

This time Max's jaw dropped. "Utah? You're kiddin' me."

"I wish. My dad left me some land there with a cabin

on it.'' He paused, another smirk altering his features. ''I've never even seen it.''

''What about that big deal we have pending? I know the Japanese are known for their patience, but—''

Even though his voice trailed off, Garth heard the panic in it. He couldn't comfort Max, because he felt the same way. To walk out and leave the corporation that he'd built from the bottom up went against the work ethic that had been drilled into him.

''Deal or no deal, what choice do I have?'' he said out loud.

Max sighed. ''None.''

''I'm going to have to depend on you more than ever. Are you up to the challenge?''

Max's face brightened, though his voice remained sober. ''I won't let you down.''

''And I won't let you down—or this company. When I get back from Dumpsville, I'll be as good as new. And that's a promise.''

Jerking his thoughts out of the past, Garth groaned as a shaft of pain shot through his skull. He walked to the window, all the while nursing the lump on the side of his head.

Damn that woman for adding to his physical misery. And double-damn her for having such a cute ass that she was making him mentally miserable, as well.

Desperate to regain control of his wandering mind, he stared out the window, concentrating on the orchard of peach trees loaded with fruit.

It was a damn shame the crop had to go to waste, he thought, just as the phone rang.

''Has something happened that we should know about?''

"Uh, why do you ask that?" Tiffany heard the uneasiness in her own voice, and knew without a doubt that Bridget had picked up on it, too, especially as they were practically able to read each other's minds.

"Hey, remember who you're talking to here, okay? You can't pull the wool over my eyes, so don't even try."

"I thought you were supposed to be concentrating on getting well?"

"My body might be in traction, but my mind isn't. So fess up."

Tiffany sighed. "All right. First, though, tell me how you're doing."

"I'm progressing about as well as the doctors predicted. It's just going to take longer than I wanted." Bridget paused. "You're not about to tell me you have to get back to Houston, are you?"

"No, though you might send me packing when *I* fess up, as you put it. If you don't, then Jeremiah might."

"Stopping beating around the bush. I'm about to have a hissy fit, and you know that's not good for me."

"I knocked Jeremiah's friend in the head." Once she'd blurted out the confession, Tiffany waited for the fireworks. She wasn't disappointed.

"*What?*"

"He's okay, really he is."

"What on earth—?"

Before Bridget could go on, Tiffany jumped in and told her the entire story. When she finished, a long silence added to her already jangled nerves. Replaying the entire scenario made it seem even more incredible than it already was.

"Oh, Tiff, how could you?" Bridget exclaimed.

"I screwed up. What more can I say?"

"Nothing. It's just so…bizarre. Well, as long as he isn't hurt, then don't worry about it." Bridget paused, then chuckled.

"What's so damn funny?"

"You, actually. I can just picture you sneaking up on that poor unsuspecting man and—"

"Okay, okay. Let's not beat a dead horse. Maybe I won't have to see him again."

"I wouldn't count on that, especially as Jeremiah was serious when he asked him to keep an eye on things around the ranch."

"Well, let's put it this way—I'll go out of my way to avoid running into him. Trust me, I'm not at the top of his friend list."

Bridget chuckled again. "I'm sure you're not, which is all the more reason why my husband should stop being so stubborn. I've tried to tell him he needs to get away from here, go back to the ranch himself and see to things."

"You can forget that. He's not about to leave you."

"I know, and I'm really glad, but still…" Bridget's voice trailed off before she changed the subject and asked, "How's Taylor? I—we miss her so much."

"She's right here, dancing a jig to talk to you both."

That conversation between the four of them had taken place two hours ago now. Since then, Tiffany had taken Taylor to a birthday party that was to last the afternoon. Once she returned to the house, she'd done a few chores, though there weren't many, as Bridget had left everything in immaculate order.

It didn't seem possible that she had been here only three days. To Tiffany, it seemed like three months, especially now, with nothing but time on her hands.

She had considered going into town, looking up Irma

Quill and introducing herself to her. But she'd nixed that idea, since she wasn't in the best of moods herself, only she didn't understand why.

Peace in Taylor's absence should be savored. Although her young charge was no trouble, she was a typical six-year-old. Tiffany wasn't used to the demands that went along with caring for a child of any age.

Still, Taylor wasn't at the root of her restlessness. Garth Dixon was the reason she couldn't settle down. God, how could she have mistaken him for a prowler, or worse? Easy. She was out of her element in these woods—plus, she had a habit of reacting before she thought.

Obviously she wouldn't be able to avoid him completely, which meant...what? Was she trying to convince herself that she should make amends? No way! She hadn't meant to hurt him. But if his reaction was the barometer by which she would be judged, she'd done it on purpose and without just cause.

Well, that was his problem, not hers. Yet she couldn't stop thinking that somehow she should at least try to cultivate some goodwill, if for no other reason than so he would be available in case of an emergency.

Tiffany tromped into the kitchen, where she paused. Maybe she should make a cake and take it to him. He had looked as if he could use some calories. Besides, hadn't the old adage that said the way to a man's heart was through his stomach proved to be true?

While she didn't give a flip about getting to his heart, she didn't have anything against satisfying his stomach.

"Then just do it and get it over with," she said out loud, crossing to the cabinets and opening them until she found a couple of mixing bowls.

An hour later, after having called Taylor at her

friend's house and found out where Garth lived, she put the cake in a plastic container and set off through the woods. By the time she arrived, Tiffany had decided she should be committed, convinced she was the last person he wanted to see.

Still, now that she'd bitten the bullet and come this far, she wasn't about to chicken out. If he didn't want to accept the cake, then he could dump it in the trash. At least she'd made the effort.

She didn't know what she was expecting in the way of a house, but certainly not what she encountered. The cabin appeared to be a dump, if the outside was any indication. The house and much of the land around it had a run-down, neglected appearance, as if the place were deserted. Despite the sunlight and the heat, Tiffany shivered.

After knocking twice and getting no response, she went around to the back of the house, where she saw a truck. She frowned as she walked up to the back door. She placed her hand on the knob and, to her surprise, the door opened.

"Yo, anybody home?"

When she got no answer, she stepped inside, only to pull up short. The place was a wreck. From where she stood, she could see into the kitchen, where dishes needed to be washed.

Her instinct was to pitch in and start cleaning, but she knew that was out of the question. If he chose to live sloppily, then so be it. It was none of her business. Trying to ignore the mess, she moved farther into the room and set the cake down on the corner of the table.

"Mr. Dixon?"

Still no response. With her curiosity getting the better of her, Tiffany tiptoed toward the living room, all the while feeling like the intruder she'd accused him of being.

Only after she saw Garth stretched out on the couch did her footsteps falter. Although she noted in passing that his face was devoid of color and that he looked thin, even thinner than she had remembered, it was his mode of dress that trapped her attention.

He had on jeans, and nothing else. She swallowed against a rising tide of heat as she took in his broad shoulders and the curling mat of hair that trailed down his stomach and lower.

She swallowed again, wondering how someone who looked so damn fit and sexy could be so ill. By looking at him, one would never know he had a bad heart. She suspected he'd caused a few, though.

Pushing that thought aside, Tiffany inched closer. That was when she saw the exhaustion in the form of circles under the heavy fringes of his lashes and etched in the lines on his face. Neither could be erased, even in sleep. He looked... Her mind floundered for words to describe him, and could come up with only one: *vulnerable.*

Even so, there was nothing soft about his features or his body. Yet, for someone whose demeanor was so compelling, he seemed lifeless, as if he...

"Garth?" she whispered, unaware that she'd frantically spoken his name.

Nothing.

Her breath caught as old questions resurfaced. Had her blow been lethal after all? Or had he had a heart attack? She bent over him, her gaze freezing on his chest.

Was he dead?

Five

She was naked.

Garth held his breath as she drifted toward him, her arms outstretched. He had never seen such a perfect body. The alabaster color of her skin made her appear so fragile that he caught his breath, while her voluptuous curves stopped the flow of saliva in his mouth, making it so dry he couldn't speak.

Her breasts were full, but taut, and her nipples reminded him of tiny rosebuds that had never opened. Her waist was dented in just enough to give her hips the provocative shape and sway that forced him to lick his parched lips while his gaze drifted over her thighs, down to her ankles.

At first he couldn't put a face with the body, but then, the closer she came, raw desire surrounding her, he knew.

Tiffany Russell.

No! That couldn't be true. It couldn't be her, unless he'd had the big one and was no longer living on this earth. Yet he felt soft fingers touch him, then nestle in the hairs on his chest.

Suddenly he opened his eyes, and his clouded blue ones locked with huge green ones. Her mouth was only a breath away from his. He heard her muted cry, but before she could make another sound, he whispered, "Shh, it's all right. I won't hurt you. You're the most beautiful thing I've ever seen."

It was then that he clasped a hand around her neck and drew her lips down to his. Greedily he drank from her mouth, which was as sensual as the rest of her, sucking on her bottom lip, then thrusting his tongue against hers. He'd never tasted anything so delicious.

Was he dreaming? Or was he for sure in heaven?

At first, Tiffany was too shocked to move. Only after she felt his tongue wrap around hers and his free hand surround a breast did she find the strength to jerk her mouth away and straighten to her full height.

"Damn you!" she cried, shoving her wild hair behind her ears and backing up, horror-stricken at what had happened. She almost slapped his face. Later, she didn't know what had stopped her. Maybe it was the pain and confusion mirrored on his face.

Garth blinked several times before his eyes opened fully once again and he stared at her. The room was suddenly charged with enough heat to scorch anything in its path.

Tiffany grappled to say something, anything, that would contain that heat, but her emotions were too chaotic and she was too furious. How dare he pull a stunt like that?

How dare she let him? In defense of herself, she'd
had no choice. Since she hadn't been able to determine
just by looking at him if he was alive, she'd had to touch
him, only to land in his arms. Damn!

Tiffany watched as Garth thrust a hand through his
already mussed hair, never taking his gaze off her.

"Would you believe me if I said I was dreaming?
That I didn't know what I was doing?"

She laughed without humor. "I wouldn't believe anything you said, actually. I think you were hell-bent on
paying me back for making mush out of your head."

"Is there anything I can say or do to convince you
otherwise?"

"No, but what you *can* do is go to hell!"

With that, Tiffany turned and stormed out of the
cabin. Halfway back to the ranch, she remembered that
she'd left the cake.

She stopped and smacked herself on the forehead.

He didn't deserve it. Maybe she should go back and
get it. No, absolutely not.

The best she could hope for was that he would choke
on it.

"When are Mommy and Daddy coming home?"

"Soon, honey, or at least, I hope so."

Tiffany stared at Taylor, who was sitting beside her
in the car. Her tiny features were pinched, which tugged
at Tiffany's heart. She was afraid it would be a while
longer before the little girl was reunited with her parents,
although Tiffany hoped to take her to the hospital as
soon as she received the green light from Bridget or
Jeremiah.

"We'll go see them soon, maybe tomorrow."

Taylor's face brightened somewhat, but then the pinched look returned. "Will my mommy walk again?"

Tiffany's stomach clenched. "Sure she will, sweetheart. She's just messed up her back, and that takes lots of time to heal."

Taylor didn't respond, and Tiffany had an idea what was going through her mind, which wasn't good. She, too, was secretly worried about her friend and her ability to heal completely, but she wasn't about to let on to Taylor.

Well, they were on their way to the store for some groceries. Maybe Irma, whom Taylor seemed to care a great deal for, would put a smile back on her face. Besides, Tiffany had decided it was time she met the other woman.

She cast another glance at her charge and saw that Taylor had pulled out her coloring book and crayons, her hands busy outlining what looked like a bluebird.

Switching her eyes back to the road, Tiffany breathed somewhat easier. If only she could be so calmly reassured about the complications in her life. Her mouth stretched into a pencil-thin line as Garth Dixon jumped to mind. Talk about complications—he was that and more. Frankly, he was a pain in the butt, one that had blindsided her.

Why had he kissed her? Had he told her the truth when he said he'd been dreaming? Of course not. What did he take her for—someone who had just fallen off a watermelon truck? Well, she had news for him. She held firm to her belief that he'd known exactly what he was doing—punishing her for whacking him over the head.

So why couldn't she dismiss him as a jerk and put him out of her mind? She knew the answer to that question, and that was what had her in such a high snit. That kiss had played havoc with her insides, turning them into mush. No man had ever taken such hot command of her lips as he had, not to mention igniting the current that had darted through her body.

Even now, she wondered what it would be like to have those lips on her body, to have—

"Stop it," she said before she thought, then cut a glance at Taylor, who had stopped coloring and was staring at her.

"Stop what?" the child asked.

"Nothing, honey. I wasn't talking to you."

"Then who were you talking to?"

Tiffany swallowed her exasperation and forced a smile. "Actually, I was chewing myself out."

Taylor was quiet for a moment, then she grinned. "Mommy does the same thing. I think that's kinda weird."

"You're right, it is. And it's a bad habit, too."

"Why are you mad at yourself?"

"Ah, we're here," Tiffany said, ignoring Taylor's question while swinging the car into the first available parking place in front of the store.

A few minutes later, Tiffany was shaking hands with Irma and smiling into her birdlike features. She was immediately drawn to this woman. "I feel as though I already know you," she said.

Irma smiled her infectious smile. "Same here. Bridget talks about you a lot."

"Probably not all good, either."

"You're wrong. She sings your praises for forcing her to come here. Otherwise, she wouldn't be married to Jeremiah."

Tiffany grinned. "She's right about that."

"So how do you like our community?"

"So far, fine, only I wish my visit could have been under different circumstances. Since it isn't, I'm glad Taylor and I are hitting it off."

They both turned to the child, who had skipped over to the candy counter and now had her nose against the glass.

"I just pray Bridget's going to be all right."

"Me too," Tiffany said.

"So how 'bout a cup of coffee?" Irma asked, on a brighter note.

Tiffany didn't want any coffee, but she did want to pick Irma's brain about Garth Dixon. Despite her efforts to dismiss him from her mind, she couldn't, which didn't make any sense to her.

"Irma—"

The rest of the words she'd been about to speak jammed in her throat as the door opened, and she watched as Garth Dixon himself sauntered across the threshold. Tiffany would have loved to pretend not to have seen him, but that wasn't possible, as she was directly in his line of vision. Still, she didn't say a word. She couldn't. She was too busy warding off the tremor that shook her body.

Irma and Taylor didn't have that problem.

"Hiya, stranger," Irma said with a wide grin, at the same time that Taylor bounded up to him.

He returned Irma's grin, then peered down at Taylor, who was gazing up at him.

"Are you still mad at Tiffany?" she asked.

Way to go, kid. Unwittingly, Tiffany's eyes locked with Garth's.

As if sensing the undercurrent between the two of them, Irma grabbed Taylor's hand and said, "Come on, let's you and me go fetch some ice cream."

Without giving the child a chance to say yes or no, Irma shuffled her off toward the back of the store.

Even when they were alone, neither Tiffany nor Garth said a word. As the tension thickened, she couldn't help but notice that despite the pallor of his skin, made more noticeable by the ugly purple lump, he appeared overpowering, and much more dangerous than ever.

Even though she knew nothing about him, except how good he tasted, she would have bet that underneath that tight rein he kept on himself, there was an uncivilized streak, a need to teeter on the edge.

Thank God he was adequately clothed this time, she thought, taking in his white cotton shirt, jeans and boots. All that was missing was the Stetson. She wondered if he had one.

"Can I buy you a cup of coffee?"

Tiffany forced herself to meet his dark gaze. "Why would you want to do that?"

"To apologize."

Her eyes widened. "You? Apologize?"

He smiled then, which instantly changed his appearance and made her knees go weak. It rearranged his features, making him more human, less uptight. Still, a smile that potent, on a rat like him, ought to be against the law.

"And to tell you that you make a helluva cake."

"So you ate it?" she asked inanely.

"Like hogs eat slop."

She laughed. She didn't want to, but she couldn't help it.

"How 'bout we go sit down?" he asked, smiling again.

Tiffany nodded, warning herself to cool it, to stay

calm, which was completely at odds with how she felt inside.

Once they were seated in the tiny café in the back of the store, each with a cup of coffee, silence was once again the dominating factor. What was wrong with her? She'd never had a problem talking to anyone about anything.

Something else her grandmother used to tell her sprang to mind, which was that she could talk the horns off a billy goat and back on. Now Tiffany couldn't think of anything to say to this man who had kissed her like she'd never been kissed before.

Dreaming? She didn't think so.

"Look, I was out of line, okay?"

Tiffany's face burned. She didn't want to discuss that kiss, but it was between them, hovering. "That's an understatement."

"I know you won't ever believe me, but I really was dreaming."

He shifted in his chair, and couldn't quite meet her eye. Good. She wanted him to squirm. No matter what the reason, he'd had no right to take advantage of her with such fervor and enthusiasm.

"Well, am I forgiven?"

Was he serious, or merely pulling her leg? Did he really care if she forgave him or not? She couldn't tell by the bland expression on his face, even though there was a twinkle of sorts in his blue eyes. Maybe she should let bygones be bygones and give him the benefit of the doubt. After all, he *was* a friend of Jeremiah's, and he would be hanging around until Bridget came home from the hospital.

"I guess I ought to ask you the same thing."

He rubbed the lump on his temple. "So you thought I was...what? A rapist?"

Her color deepened, but she didn't flinch, though she did have the urge to put a matching lump on the other temple, especially as his smile had now turned into something suspiciously like a smirk.

"You know how it is, living in the big city. It makes you distrust everyone."

"I accept."

"What?"

He grinned. "Your apology, of course."

He was teasing her outright now, and it felt good. Maybe he was even flirting with her; that felt good, too. Whoa, girl, put the brakes on, she thought. This man could give her something that Clorox couldn't take out—a broken heart.

When she remained quiet, he went on. "Jeremiah called."

Tiffany's mouth turned down. "I suspected as much."

The twinkle in his eyes deepened, but she ignored it, refusing to take the bait. "I understand you haven't been here long," she said instead, forcing the conversation back on an even keel.

"That's right."

She heard the cautious note in his tone, but that didn't stop her. "So where're you from?"

"Texas."

"I figured as much, but since you don't wear a Stetson, I couldn't be sure."

He laughed outright, which again did something crazy to her insides.

"Actually, my hat's hanging on a nail in the closet."

"Ah, a true Texan after all. So what brings you here?"

His face closed. For a moment she thought he wasn't going to answer. "My health. I'm sure you know by now that I have a bad heart. I'm supposed to be taking it easy." He paused. "That's why my place is such a mess."

"You don't have to apologize to me for that."

"I wasn't. I was just stating a fact."

It was uncanny that he knew just which buttons to push to rile her. But no way would she let him guess that.

"So what about you?" he said into the ensuing silence. "From your accent, I'm guessing you're from the South, as well."

· "You're right. I'm also from Texas. Houston, to be exact."

"Ah, so we're both transplanted Texans."

"It's only temporary for me."

"So how long have you known the Davises?"

Tiffany smiled, then found herself telling him about her long friendship with Bridget, followed by the details of the auction and their subsequent marriage.

By the time she finished, his jaw was sagging. "You're puttin' me on."

"No, I'm not. At the time, I was just as shocked as you are now."

"Why didn't you join in the bidding?"

Tiffany gave him an incredulous look. "Me? You've got to be kidding?"

"Why? After all, it was your idea, or so you said."

"It was, only I had—*have*—no desire to be stuck permanently in this place."

"Ah, so you like the city."

"Yep, I'm a curb-and-gutter girl, and I don't apologize for it."

"Unlike your friend, farm and ranch life's definitely not for you."

"Nope. And marrying a sodbuster isn't, either. I'm a woman on the move. My goal is to own my own clothing store."

"And I bet it's safe to say you're looking for a man with money to marry, as well."

"You got it. As my grandma always said, you can love a rich one as easily as a poor one." While this was not true, Garth didn't have to know that. She had to protect herself against him.

He didn't say anything for a minute, then he stood, contempt having replaced the smile. "Well, good luck. Hope you find what you're looking for."

Following those tersely spoken words, he strode out of the store.

Six

"Bashed anyone else in the head lately?"

"Funny." Although Tiffany threw Jeremiah a sharp look, her mouth twitched, wanting to smile. "I'll never live that down, will I?"

"Oh, maybe someday," Bridget put in, sitting up in her hospital bed, her wan features stretched in a grin as she winked at Tiffany.

When Tiffany talked to Jeremiah last evening, he'd told her that Bridget was up to seeing Taylor, that the pain associated with the traction had lessened somewhat.

Early this morning, she and Taylor had left for Vegas. Now they were gathered around Bridget's bed in a room brightened by a scattering of potted plants and two bouquets of freshly cut flowers.

Still, Tiffany was concerned about her friend, whose legs didn't seem to be responding as well as the doctors had hoped. As a result, a full recovery seemed farther in the future than they'd expected, which added to Tiffany's concern. She couldn't stay in Utah indefinitely.

Yet she couldn't desert her friend, either. She would just have to take it one day at a time and keep her fingers crossed that things would work out, mainly for Bridget. The thought of her friend in a wheelchair didn't bear thinking about. She *wouldn't* think about it.

"I told you my daddy was going to be mad at you," Taylor said, cutting into the short silence.

"Why, Taylor Davis, that wasn't a nice thing to say." Jeremiah reached for his daughter and plopped her down on his knee, nuzzling her neck.

She squirmed. "That tickles."

"I'm going to tickle something else—your fanny—if you say anything like that to Tiffany again."

Tiffany batted her hand through air. "It's no biggie. Garth told me you called him. I don't mind being raked over the coals."

This time Bridget laughed, facing her husband. "I warned you that she had a smart mouth."

"That you did, love," Jeremiah said, looking at his wife as if he could eat her.

Tiffany felt an instant and deep twinge of jealousy. No one had ever looked at her like that, except maybe in that split second when Garth grabbed her. Realizing the track her mind had taken, she cursed silently, then forced herself to concentrate on what Jeremiah was saying.

"I'm not mad, Tiff. Surely you know that. I just wanted to make sure Garth was all right, and that he'd continue to see about the two of you and the ranch. I wasn't sure he would, after—"

Tiffany cut in with a reluctant smile. "I get the picture. He was plenty mad enough to renege."

"Boy, that's right," Taylor said. "They got it on."

Bridget threw her stepdaughter a look. "'Got it on'? Where on earth did you pick up that expression?"

"At school."

Bridget and Jeremiah rolled their eyes. Tiffany laughed. "That's right, kid. You just told the truth. We did get it on, though just verbally."

"So is Garth really okay?" Jeremiah asked, his tone serious. "I don't know all that much about him, except that he has a bad heart."

"And a bad temper," Tiffany muttered. "But I know what you mean," she added hurriedly, so as not to sound too callous. "He's okay. His pride seems to have taken the brunt of the effects."

"Good." Jeremiah tousled his daughter's hair. "How 'bout the two of us going to the cafeteria and leaving these women to yak?"

Taylor lunged off his lap, grabbed his hand and pulled him toward the door. "Can I have a jelly roll?"

When they had gone, Tiffany turned to Bridget. "You have a wonderful family. A few minutes ago, I was envying you that."

Bridget twisted a copper-colored curl as she cocked her head, her eyes serious. "You could have the same thing, you know, *if* you weren't so independent and pigheaded."

"Now is that any way to talk to a friend?"

"Yes, especially when it's the truth." Bridget grinned. "The thought did enter my mind that maybe you and our neighbor might hit it off." Her grin exploded into full-fledged laughter. "No pun intended, of course."

"Of course," Tiffany said, her tone rich with sarcasm.

"Okay, so you're not interested. But you have to admit, he's a piece of eye candy."

"Only problem is, I happen not to like that flavor," Tiffany said in a rush.

Bridget merely looked at her, then changed the subject. "All right, I'll stop meddling. So tell me what you plan to do when I get home and you go back to your real life? I know you want to open a store of your own."

Tiffany smiled. "Ah, now that's something I love to talk about."

Two days had passed since that run-in with Garth at the store and her subsequent visit to the hospital. And though she hadn't seen him again, Tiffany felt certain he'd been around, having given his word to Jeremiah.

She figured he'd come when she and Tiffany were either in town or at the park. She'd done her best to keep the child occupied. So far, she was proud of her babysitting abilities.

Now, however, Taylor was out playing, and she was alone in a house that was spotless and stocked with more cooked food than either of them could eat. In a nutshell, she was bored. Maybe what she needed was another sparring match with Garth Dixon to liven things up. She scoffed out loud.

He was avoiding her, probably because she'd insulted him with her knee-jerk statement about not wanting to marry a sodbuster, which was exactly what he was. Would she ever learn *not* to speak her mind? She really hadn't meant to insult him; the words had just popped out.

Still, she had no intention of spending the rest of her life living hand to mouth, working the dirt and rounding up cattle, which was exactly what Garth would be doing.

He would remain on his land, such as it was, and continually sweat over where the money for his next meal was coming from.

He hadn't said as much, but her gut instinct said she was right. What a waste of manhood, she told herself, remembering how his lips had set her on fire. But she would just have to douse that raging fire with a dose of sound reality. While it was a given that every time they were together they set off sexual fireworks, she knew it would be stupid to let herself feel anything for the man.

Again, and unlike Bridget, she could never adapt to living here, especially with someone who was not only ill, but cantankerous to boot. So why couldn't she stop thinking about him and that kiss?

Unwilling to answer that question, Tiffany shook off thoughts of Garth and walked outside to the porch, where her heart plunged to her toes. Taylor was halfway up a tree whose limbs were too flimsy even for someone of her light weight.

"Taylor, no!" Tiffany hollered, then bounded off the porch. "Get down this second!"

"Why?" Taylor asked, clinging to a branch that was even now beginning to split.

"Because I said so!"

"Yes, ma'am."

Still afraid Taylor was in danger, Tiffany began running toward her. By the time she was halfway there, Taylor, apparently sensing she was in trouble, swung to the ground.

But because Tiffany had eyes only for her charge, she didn't watch where she was stepping—until it was too late. Without warning, both feet flew out from under her.

Splat!

Her rear end hit the ground—hard. She realized where

she'd landed even before the stench surrounded her—
right in the middle of a pile of wet cow manure.

Garth walked through the orchard, his forehead wrin-
kling in a frown as he stopped and stared at a tree loaded
with luscious-smelling peaches. He reached up and
plucked one, and without so much as wiping it off, bit
into it.

That was when *her* face jumped to the forefront of his
mind. A curse exploded from his lips. Tiffany Russell
was the last person he wanted to think about.

He shook his head, but the vision of her wouldn't go
away. Since he first met her, she'd been nothing but a
first-class pain in the butt. To make matters worse, he'd
gone off the deep end and kissed her. But how the hell
had he known the subject of his dream would invade his
privacy, then have the gall to sneak up on him and touch
his chest?

Unreal.

He shouldn't have been surprised. Hell, she'd knocked
him halfway to Texas and back. Why should he have
been surprised at anything else she did? He hadn't been,
but still, he couldn't seem to stop thinking about her—
or that kiss.

He took another bite of the peach, then licked the juice
off a finger, suddenly wishing it was Tiffany's lips he
was licking instead.

Cursing, he threw the peach as far as he could. He
had come here to heal his body and his mind, not to
become tangled in any more problems. And Tiffany Russell was definitely a problem.

His mouth formed a half smile as he forced himself
to admit that he couldn't help but admire her honesty

and her spunk. She'd told him right out that ranchers and farmers were not for her.

Well, he was no rancher or farmer, but she didn't know that. And it didn't matter. A woman with an attitude and a mouth as big as Texas wasn't for him. Still, to his dying day, he would never find anyone who looked better in jeans than she did.

Just thinking about her derriere and how it would feel to touch it made him grunt in self-disgust, even as he became instantly aroused.

Cursing again, he headed back toward the cabin, vowing to stay the hell away from her, even though he knew that wasn't possible.

He reached the porch just as the phone rang. Another frown creased his face. He didn't want to talk on the phone. He wanted to take a cold shower, since he was still painfully aroused.

Thinking that it was his family checking on him, he made a mad dash for the receiver, but the caller turned out to be his assistant, Max. Even as he asked Max what he wanted, Garth found himself breathless with excitement. Until he heard Max's voice, he hadn't realized just how *much* he missed his work.

Would this nightmare ever end? He still couldn't understand how someone with his zest and stamina could have a heart condition in the first place. Even now, with Max in Dallas and him in Utah, it didn't seem possible.

"If your doctors knew I was calling you," Max was saying, "they'd have what little hide I've got left."

"Hey, buddy, don't worry about that. I'll take care of them. I'm damn glad you called."

"That remains to be seen."

"So what's wrong? I can tell from your voice that it's serious." Garth's mind raced. Any number of important deals were pending, not to mention the one with the Japanese. Any one of them could be headed for the toilet.

"The Japanese are getting impatient. In fact, they're squealing."

"I was hoping that wasn't the case, but I'm not surprised."

"Any quick and easy suggestions from Boonieville?"

Garth knew Max was trying to make light of the situation to lessen the stress on him. Unfortunately for the company and for him personally, there was no way to do that.

"Look," Max said into the ensuing silence, "I shouldn't have bothered you. Forget I called, okay? I'll think—"

"Give it a rest, will you? My ticker's not the problem right now. It's holding up fine. It's my mind that's on the rampage."

"Mine, too. They said they'd give us ninety days. Now they're crawfishing."

"Well, you tell them I'm holding them to their word. Do you know what spooked them?"

"I don't think it's your condition, but it might be. Or they may have rummaged up a better deal."

"There is no better deal," Garth snapped. "Just keep me posted on this one."

"Will do."

After he hung up, Garth felt more restless than ever. He hated being a damn invalid. He should be in the office, where he damn well wanted to be and where he belonged.

Clenching his teeth, he grabbed his Stetson and walked to the door, only to stop as the phone rang again. Surely that wasn't Max calling him back so soon.

It wasn't, though as soon as he answered he wished it was.

"How the hell did you get this number?"

After listening for a few minutes longer, he lashed out. "Leave me the hell alone. Don't *ever* call here again!"

An hour later, he was still seething over the call. Deciding to put his restless energy to good use, he would go check on Tiffany and Taylor.

By the time he reached the Davis place, his temper and his heart rate had cooled, especially when he walked into the backyard in time to see Tiffany slip in cow muck.

He leaned up against a tree and drawled, "Well, well, what have we here?"

Without getting up, Tiffany swung around. "It's not funny," she snapped.

"Who's laughing?"

"You!"

"Me too," Taylor chimed in.

"I think I hear Piper Girl meowing," Tiffany said, gritting her teeth.

Without another word, the child skipped toward the barn.

Garth crossed his arms over his chest, his lips twitching. Only after Taylor disappeared did he say, "I remember someone once told me that it's always dangerous to throw mud, that you never know when some of it might stick to your own rear."

"Damn you!"

"However, in your case, it's not mud." He grinned outright. "It's cow dung."

Tiffany glowered at him. "I told you, this is not funny! *You're* not funny."

His grin didn't slip one iota as he watched her struggle

to get up, her efforts in vain. The splattering of the manure made it impossible for her to regain her footing.

"Want some help?" he asked, ambling toward her.

"No! I don't want you to touch me. What I do want is for you to leave me the hell alone."

"No problem."

"And you're not welcome on this property, either!"

Garth's grin widened as he turned and sauntered off. "See ya."

Seven

"**R**ead me another one."

Tiffany looked at her watch, then shook her left foot, which had gone to sleep. "Not now, sweetie. There's not time."

She had been sitting on the couch for the past hour, reading ghost short stories to Taylor.

"Please, just one more," Taylor whined, snuggling closer to Tiffany's side.

Tiffany peered into her upturned face. "Hey, haven't you forgotten something?"

Taylor looked puzzled.

"Your swimming lessons start today. Remember?"

"Oh, cool!" Taylor bounced off the couch. "Are you taking me?"

Tiffany gave her charge a light pinch on the cheek, then smiled. "Know what? I think you're getting early Alzheimer's."

"What's Al—"

"Forget it," Tiffany said, rising from the couch herself. "And no, I'm not taking you. Mrs. McNair and Martha are picking you up. And you're supposed to spend the night with Martha. She's having a slumber party. You're the young one here. You're supposed to remember all those things."

Taylor merely laughed, then raced toward her room. "Oh, boy! I finally get to wear my new bathing suit Mommy bought me." She paused, then swung around, her lower lip trembling. "I want my mommy. She—"

"Hey, it's going to be all right. *She's* going to be all right." Tiffany crossed the room and gave the child a hug. "It's going to take time, that's all." Tiffany forced a confident smile. "Just think what a big surprise you'll have for Mommy and Daddy when they get home. I'm counting on you to be the best swimmer in the class. That'll make 'em real proud."

As she pulled away, Taylor's quiver turned into a watery smile. "Think I can swim good?"

"Of course you can, kiddo. With your long arms and legs, you'll be a whiz in that water." Tiffany gestured toward the bedroom. "Hurry now, and hop into that suit. Your friend will be here any moment."

Fifteen minutes later, Taylor ran out the door, her small bag swinging from her hand, and climbed into the McNairs' car. Tiffany stood on the front porch and watched until all she could see was dust.

Turning, she walked back into the house, where she simply stood in the middle of the living room for a long moment, suddenly wondering what on earth she was going to do with the remainder of the afternoon.

She had never been wild about kids, never thought she would want any. But somehow Taylor had managed to worm her way into her heart and make her think that maybe there might be more to life than a career.

"Get a grip, woman," she murmured, ridiculing herself for becoming maudlin. The last thing she needed was to be responsible for someone other than herself. Hell, right now she didn't even have a job!

Tiffany laughed out loud. More to the point, she didn't have a husband, or even a prospect of one. And while she might not need a husband to make a baby, she did need a man, which was something she didn't have, either.

Shaking her head to clear it of those unwanted thoughts, she marched into the kitchen, deciding to make a loaf of sweet-potato bread. Although cooking was far from her favorite thing, she felt she had to at least make an effort for Taylor's sake. She needed at least one hot meal a day. With that thought in mind, Tiffany made her way to the sink.

She was washing her hands when she saw him. Her stomach tightened as she watched Garth stride toward the barn. She forced out her pent-up breath, but that did nothing to loosen the knot in her belly.

She wished she had the answer to why this particular man affected her this way. One minute his presence set her body on fire, and the next minute he made her mad enough to take another swing at his head.

Oh, to hell with him, she thought, her mouth tightening. She had tried her best not to dwell on the incident in the yard. She'd made it a point not to go anywhere near the barn, for fear of running into him.

But even now, two days later, she could still hear his laughter, could still see that smirk on his face as she'd struggled to get her footing so she could get out of that pile of cow dung.

Taylor hadn't helped, either. She'd laughed until she got a stitch in her side.

Suddenly Tiffany's stomach clenched with an emotion of a different kind—the urge to throw up again as the details of that afternoon resurfaced. Once she'd gotten up and made her way to the porch, she'd lost the contents of her stomach, even before she could shed her disgusting cutoffs.

Instead of washing them, she'd opted to bag them and toss them in the garbage, his laughter continuing to ring in her ears all the while. Her humiliation deepening, she'd wished she'd had the nerve to slap that laughter off his face. But after already nearly scrambling his brain with the shovel, she'd decided not to push her luck.

Besides, she hadn't been able to wait to rid herself of that ghastly scent. She'd taken a shower and scrubbed her body until it was nearly raw.

Now, as she looked on as Garth went about his business, seemingly without so much as a glance in the direction of the house, she felt her resentment and anger rise all over again.

Fine. Two could play this game. Anyway, she was far too attracted to this stranger. Something needed to give. She was glad he had rejected her. Pride and sound judgment would force her to do the same.

If only she wasn't so curious about him. He seemed to have two different sides, which intrigued her. Something about him indicated that he had a lot of breeding, even though he dressed and acted as if he didn't have a pot to pee in or a window to throw it out of.

What was wrong with her? She didn't care what he had or didn't have. It had no bearing on her. She didn't want a man in her life. She wanted a career. And the sooner she got back to civilization, the sooner she could get started on that. Obviously this place and the enforced idleness were working on her psyche—and not in a good way, either.

Jerking her eyes off Garth, Tiffany reached down to open the cabinet beneath the sink. "Oh, no!" she cried, watching as water seeped from under the closed doors.

She grabbed a knob, jerked one side open, then stared in horror at a gushing pipe.

"Swell! Just swell!" she snapped, frantically groping for the drawer filled with kitchen towels. Her efforts were too little, too late. The situation was already out of control.

Surrounded by water, she surged to her feet, her mind groping for a solution. Common sense told her that she should turn off the water at the main, but she didn't know where that was—or even if there was such a thing as a main, way out here in the country.

Then it hit her. Garth. Was he still around? She looked out the window again and saw him. Thank God. She raced outside, onto the porch.

Having apparently heard the door open, Garth glanced in her direction at the same time she bounded down the steps.

"What's the matter?" he asked without preamble, starting toward her.

She met him halfway, out of breath. "The pipe, under the sink—it's gushing water. Can you stop it?"

"Won't know till I take a look."

"Hurry, before it floods the whole house."

"Let's go." Garth tossed aside the oily rag in his hand and followed her indoors.

Twenty minutes later Tiffany was standing anxiously by, observing, while he labored under the sink. She'd found the correct tools in the utility/storage room. As a result of his labor, the water was no longer gushing, but he hadn't as yet been able to completely plug the leak.

"Dammit!" he muttered.

"Are you sure there's nothing I can do to help?" This wasn't the first time she'd asked that question, and she got the same answer as before.

"No. I think I just about have it."

His determination to complete the repair alone gave her no choice but to stand idly by, which was the problem, especially when her eyes were filled with nothing but his backside.

She shifted from one bare foot to the other, trying not to look, then finding herself doing just that. And enjoying the hell out of it, too.

His tush was major-league. No doubt about it. As a rule, his jeans were always a bit baggy. She suspected that stemmed from his recent illness. Now, however, with him hunched over, on his knees, under the cabinet, his tush was clearly defined.

Tiffany licked her lips and fought off the sudden urge to run a finger along that tempting curve. For a moment, the urge almost got the better of her. Averting her gaze, she stiffened. Still, the image lingered, and her skin tingled as a funny feeling that started in her stomach worked its way down until she felt a flush of heat between her legs.

This time she couldn't move, her torrid emotions holding her captive. She had never in her life felt such a powerful physical attraction for a man, and it scared the hell out of her.

Besides knowing he had no money and seemingly no ambition, she didn't know a damn thing about him, except that he turned her on sexually. To think that moments ago she'd wanted to run her finger down his buttocks...

More mortified than ever at her thoughts, Tiffany turned back around just as he moved. Terrific, she groaned inwardly as another jolt from the hot needle of sexual attraction surged through her.

"Hey, you still willing to help?"

She cleared her throat. "Of course."

"Then get down here and grab hold of this pipe while I try to tighten it. The damn thing keeps slipping."

She did as she was told, only to find herself in even more trouble. When her fingers surrounded the pipe, she was so close to him that she could feel his breath on her cheek, not to mention smelling the scent of sweat mixed with a touch of cologne.

She ached to squirm as she felt another burst of that hot excitement. If she so much as turned a fraction...

Only she *wouldn't* turn, she assured herself, forcing herself to stare straight ahead, concentrating on a tiny hole in the back wall of the cabinet.

The best way to come out of this entire episode unscathed was not to let him know how he affected her. God forbid he should get even the slightest hint that she was attracted to him.

"That's it," he murmured. "Keep holding on."

"I'm trying."

"You're doing just fine."

"Can you fix it?" she asked, still staring straight ahead as she gripped the cold metal.

He didn't answer, but what he did do was move his arm suddenly, which positioned it against the soft curve of her breast.

She heard his indrawn breath just as her own breathing turned ragged and her heart slapped her chest.

Heat, hot and fast, rushed between them.

"Tiffany," he whispered.

That harsh, shaky note in his voice drew her eyes to his. She tried to read the expression in them, but she could see only the raw desire and feel the raw sexual energy that connected them, refusing to let go.

"Garth—" Further words dried up in her throat as he leaned closer.

She knew he was going to kiss her again, and there wasn't a damn thing she could do to stop it. And the worst thing about it was that she didn't want to.

Eight

He heard her pounding heart, saw the wildness in her expression, and knew that he would rather be tarred and feathered than turn away from the hot invitation in her eyes.

But he had to resist. If he ever once touched her the way he wanted to, then... His body tensed, and he began to pull back, but then suddenly, he felt a hand behind his neck. He told himself that her action couldn't be a deliberate provocation, but he knew it was. What else could it be? Her hand was like a vise, pulling him closer.

"What are you trying to do to me?" he muttered thickly, knowing, but realizing that it didn't matter. Whether he liked it or not, he'd had it.

His lips landed against hers with unerring accuracy, and when his hot tongue invaded her mouth, he realized that he'd more than had it, he was lost. Damned.

Her deep moan turned his desire into sheer lust as his

hand moved up and down her spine, then came around to cover a full breast. He felt her tremble, which spread that lust through him like a raging fire.

He wanted to take her on the spot, under the damn wet cabinet, frantic to relieve the mounting pain in his groin.

Only he wasn't going to. Not now, not ever. He couldn't allow himself to get involved. "God, Tiffany, no," he said, pushing her away.

For a moment, she appeared too stunned to move. Then she scrambled out from under the cabinet and stood with her back to him. When he followed suit, the silence in the room built to a lethal pitch.

"You can go now," she said, her voice low and raspy. "You're no longer needed."

"Look, Tiffany, I—"

"Save it for someone who gives a damn," she said, making her way toward the door.

"Hey, you can't just walk off like that."

She stopped and swung around, her eyes flashing. "I can do anything I damn well please."

With that she thrust open the screen door and stormed outside. Jamming his hands down into his pockets, he stood at the window and tracked her until she reached the fence at the far end of the yard. Once there, she stopped and leaned against a post.

Cursing, Garth stormed out the door himself, following in her footsteps, without a clue as to what he was going to say to her. But he knew he had to say something. Part of this skirmish was his fault. Granted, she had initiated the kiss, but he'd jumped in headfirst, and he hadn't wanted to stop.

When he reached her side, she visibly stiffened, while continuing to stare straight ahead.

"Go away," she said in a listless tone.

He didn't budge. He owed her an explanation. Only now that he was here, he wasn't prepared to give her one. He wasn't prepared to leave her, either, which was a hell of a predicament. He glanced sideways at her, and at the same time the wind doused him with her scent, the scent of roses. God, she smelled good. And to make matters worse, she looked good.

She was standing ramrod-straight, her golden hair caressing the side of one cheek. But it failed to hide a heart-shaped face that needed no makeup to look breathtakingly lovely. He couldn't take his eyes off her.

Yet there was nothing flashy about her, as had been the case with all the other women in his life. This one had an earthiness, a boldness, that drew her to him.

Whatever the reason, he had the sense to know he was in deep trouble, especially as he was so hard that only getting dog-sucking drunk would cure him.

"It was just a kiss, you know," she said, quietly and out of the blue.

"Just a kiss, huh?"

"Yes."

"That's wishful thinking—on both our parts. And you know it."

She cut him a sharp glance, her chin jutting out. "In spite of what you think—"

"What I think is that if we hadn't been under that damn sink, we'd have screwed right there in the middle of all that water on the kitchen floor."

Tiffany's eyes flashed. "Only in your dreams!"

"Look, this is getting us nowhere."

"You're right, and that's exactly where we're going— you and me—*nowhere.*"

Garth rammed his fingers through his hair. "I never

said we were. So where do you suggest we go from here? I'm not going to shirk my duty. I promised to look after things around the place."

"Fine, but just stay out of my way."

"Don't forget—you kissed me."

She flushed and turned away.

"And believe me, I enjoyed every minute of it," Garth said with a terse gentleness. "In fact, I'd like nothing better than to continue where we left off, here, in the wide-open spaces, with you on top—"

"Stop it!" Tiffany stepped away from him, her face suffused with color. "I don't know what came over me, what I was thinking about. Anyway, as I said, it was just a kiss. I—"

Suddenly her voice broke, and a funny look came over her face.

"What's wrong?" Garth demanded.

"Over there!" She pointed beyond his shoulder, toward a far corner of the pasture. "Is that what I think it is?"

Garth turned, squinted, then shifted his gaze back to her. "Damn sure is. It's a calf."

"Tangled in barbed wire?"

"Yep."

"Oh, God," Tiffany whispered.

"Go, go…" Garth pushed her ahead of him, and they both started to run.

By the time they reached the animal, they were both out of breath, especially Garth. He felt like a junkie who'd run out of amphetamines.

"Are you all right?" Tiffany asked, albeit not in a warm tone.

"Other than having a bad ticker and being old to boot,

hell, I'm in tip-top shape.'' His sarcasm almost drew a smile, he noticed.

"You're not *that* old."

"Thanks."

This time she did chuckle, just as he knelt beside the struggling calf. Momentarily he felt her beside him, and he watched as she placed her hand on the animal's head.

"Poor baby," she cooed. "You just hold on, you hear? Garth's going to get you out of this mess."

The unexpected use of his name jolted him. But then, everything about this woman jolted him. "She's right, little fellow."

"He's cut on his backside!" Tiffany cried suddenly.

Garth had already seen the blood, but he hadn't said anything. "You hold him as still as you can while I pull the barbed wire out."

"Please, don't hurt him, okay?" Tiffany's voice sounded small now, as she concentrated on doing as he'd asked.

"I'll be as gentle as I can."

Ten minutes later, Garth lifted the animal in his arms and toted him into the barn.

"Shouldn't we take him to the vet?" Tiffany asked, falling to her knees on the hay next to the calf.

"Nah. I can dress his wounds. They're not that deep."

Garth proceeded to do just that, all the while feeling her eyes following his every move. When he'd finished and the animal was settled, he looked across at her, and again their eyes locked for an intense moment.

She broke contact first and looked away.

"Thanks for your help," he said, for lack of anything better to say, feeling her strong physical pull once again.

She faced him. "You seem to have a way with animals. With all that land you have, I find it strange that you don't have some cattle of your own.''

Garth rose, then said, in a rougher tone than he'd intended, ''I'm not interested.''

''Just what are you interested in?'' Before he could answer, she shook her head, then held up her hand. ''Forget I asked. It's none of my business, and besides, I don't really care.''

Before he could find a suitable comeback, she was already out of the barn. For the second time in one day, he stood helplessly by and watched the swing of her buttocks.

Gritting his teeth, Garth fought the renewed urge to return to his cabin and get flat-out drunk.

''You be a good girl now, you hear?''

Taylor wrinkled her nose. ''I'm always a good girl.''

''Yeah, sure you are,'' Tiffany said with a grin, before leaning over and planting a kiss on the child's cheek. ''Like the time you climbed that tree and almost busted your keester.''

''What's a keester?''

''Your rear.''

Taylor laughed. ''*You're* the one who did that.''

''Don't remind me.'' Tiffany's smile was lame at best.

They had just driven up Lilah Davis's driveway. Jeremiah's aunt had called and practically begged to keep Taylor for a few days, saying that her leg, which had been temporarily paralyzed from her stroke, was much better, and that the doctor was now letting her drive.

Lilah had gone on to say that she had discussed Taylor's visit with Jeremiah and Bridget and they had consented, but only if she, Tiffany, didn't mind staying by herself at the ranch. Tiffany had to admit that, although she would miss Taylor, she definitely wasn't afraid to stay alone.

Now, as she watched Lilah Davis walk onto her front porch, she and Taylor scrambled out of the car at the same time.

"I'm pleased to meet you," Lilah said, after hugging her great-niece, then shaking Tiffany's outstretched hand. "It's about time we met, young lady. Bridget talks about you all the time."

"Same here," Tiffany said, smiling at a woman who looked the way everybody's grandmother ought to look—rosy-cheeked, slightly overweight and as sweet as the goodies she made.

"I hope you have time to come in for coffee and tea cakes."

"Thanks, but no thanks," Tiffany said, staring at the sky. "According to the weather report, a storm's brewing. When I come back after Taylor, I'll take you up on that offer."

"I'll hold you to that."

After giving Taylor another quick hug, she left, only to find herself, hours later, rambling around the house like a lost goose. Without Taylor's active presence, the place was just too quiet. Tomorrow she planned to drive to the hospital and spend as much of the day as possible with Bridget.

But that was tomorrow, and this was now. She had to get through the evening. Maybe she would work on updating her résumé. Soon she would have to test the job market again. Push was fast coming to shove. After making herself a cup of flavored coffee, Tiffany sat down on the couch in the living room. She had taken two sips when she heard the first loud clap of thunder.

She jumped, sloshing hot coffee over her arm.

"Darn!" she muttered, mopping up the mess with a Kleenex. She was as skittish as the calf that had gotten tangled in the barbed wire.

Groaning, she leaned back against the cushion. Thinking about that incident brought something else to mind— or rather, some*one* else. She didn't want to think about Garth Dixon and the last time they'd been together, which was three days ago.

Suddenly she felt herself turn red from the top of her head to her toes. How could she have behaved in such a brazen manner? She would admit she was oftentimes pushy and in-your-face, but never with men.

So why now? Why with this stranger? Was it because he was just that—a stranger, and a mysterious one? Was that the crux of his charm? Unfortunately, there was more. She liked the way he looked. She liked the way he smelled. She liked the way his hot lips had taken possession of hers and made her ache for more.

Thank God he had stopped, because she wasn't sure she would have. Now, though, she wasn't at all sure she could ever look him in the eye again.

Refusing to nurse that unsettling thought, she reached for her briefcase, just as the lights suddenly flickered. She grimaced. That was all she needed, with twilight approaching. Candles. Surely Bridget kept some around for emergencies. Getting up, she made her way into the utility room and rummaged through drawer after drawer. She was on the last one when the lights went out completely.

Great! Now what? Before sight became impossible, she continued to dig until she located two candles. She returned to the living room to be greeted by the ringing of the phone.

It was Garth. Her breathing turned ragged.

"I'm assuming your power's out," he said.

He sounded so normal, so blasé, as if nothing had happened between them. Because nothing *had* happened, she assured herself, mentally kicking her backside. Like she'd told him, it was just another kiss—no big deal. Only it *was* a big deal, at least to her, and that was what galled her.

"You're right, it is," she said, matching his coolness.

"Are you afraid?"

Not of the weather. "No."

"Are you sure?"

She sighed. "Yes, I'm sure."

"You don't have to snap my head off."

"I wasn't aware that I had."

Silence.

"Dammit, woman, you'd try the patience of a saint." He paused. "Look, I didn't call to argue with you. I just wanted to make sure you and Taylor were okay."

"Taylor's not here."

"Oh?"

"I took her to her aunt's for a few days."

"I see."

Another silence.

"I appreciate your calling and checking on me," she finally said. "But I'm all right."

"Why don't you come to my place?"

No way, Bubba. "What good would that do? You don't have lights, either."

"As a matter of fact, I do. I have an emergency generator that kicked in when the lights went out."

"Lucky you."

"Tiffany—"

"Thanks again, but I believe I'll stay put."

"Fine. You do just that."

He was angry, she knew, which made him even harder to figure out. He seemed to want her, yet he didn't. Nothing made sense anymore.

Vowing not to think about him for another second, Tiffany plopped back down on the couch and closed her eyes. She must have fallen asleep, because when she awakened, it was an hour later. The weather hadn't settled, nor had the lights come back on.

Getting up, she made her way to the window, only to quickly step aside as lightning flashed, seemingly just beyond the window. She rubbed her chest, feeling as if it had been singed.

That was when she made up her mind. She didn't stop to think about her decision, either. She just did it. Only after she parked the car behind his truck did she ask herself if she'd lost her mind. Not bothering to answer that question, she made a mad dash for the porch.

She knocked several times, loud. Then, getting no response, she opened the door and walked inside.

"Garth?"

No answer, which reminded her of the other time she'd come here—the first time he'd kissed her. That thought almost made her turn and run, but at the moment she was more frightened of the storm than she was of him. She could handle him; Mother Nature was a different story.

"Garth?" she called again.

He didn't answer, but she knew he was there. She saw a light and heard noise from what she assumed was his bedroom.

"Garth?"

Then, standing in the doorway, she saw why he hadn't answered her. He was in the bathroom, *in the shower*.

Oh, dear Lord, she thought, scrambling to reverse her

steps. She wasn't quick enough. The door to the shower opened, and he stepped out, naked as the day he was born.

She covered her mouth at the same time that he looked up and saw her.

Nine

"Hi.**"**

Although that tiny word came out sounding rough, as if his throat had been brushed with sandpaper, the expression in his eyes was anything but rough. A glint of hot desire sprang into them as he and Tiffany stared at one another.

Tiffany wanted to bolt, but she couldn't. Her legs felt as if they were encased in blocks of concrete. She wanted to stammer that this was a mistake, that she shouldn't be here, but she couldn't manage to do that, either. The chance to see his naked body still glistening with moisture was simply too much temptation, too much pleasure, to resist.

However, when he ventured toward her, brazen in his nakedness, panic wrapped its fingers around her heart and squeezed. That was when something inside her seemed to turn loose and she was able to move.

She took two steps back. He took two steps forward.

"I..." Tiffany began, licking her dry lips.

"It's all right." Garth's rough voice was now a whisper.

She shook her head, while continuing to edge backward.

"Please," he said in a pleading tone.

"Please what?" she couldn't help but ask.

"Don't go."

Blood rushed to her face. "I...I have to."

"Why?"

"Just because." She had to get control of herself. Here she was, babbling like an idiot, like someone who had never seen a man naked. She had, though she had to admit, it had been a long time ago, and his body hadn't looked anything like Garth's.

He had to be every woman's fantasy. Tall and slender, but with just the right amount of honed muscle, which was evident not only on his upper body, but on the rest of him, as well. His stomach looked like an old-time washboard, glistening now with beads of water.

She ached to drop her gaze, convinced that the red-hot desire in his eyes was also evident elsewhere.

"It's all right, you know," he said, closing more of the gap between them.

"What?" Her voice was barely audible.

"To look."

"Garth, please, don't." It was her turn to plead, but Tiffany knew her plea had fallen on deaf ears, for he kept on coming.

"You know you want me."

"No."

"Yes. You want me as much as I want you. It's been that way since that first time I kissed you."

"This is crazy."

"I'll *go* crazy if I can't have you." He dropped his eyes. "See for yourself."

As if she had lost control of her body, she lowered her eyes, only to jerk them back up again, blood stinging her cheeks anew.

"Convinced?"

Fire still raged in those dark, compelling eyes, but now something else was there, as well—a challenge. He was challenging her to deny what he'd just said. She couldn't, and he knew it.

Besides, he was right. To have sex with him was what she'd wanted, too, only she hadn't even realized that until now, until he'd voiced that challenge.

Her gaze dropped again, deliberately this time, to his hardness, where it lingered. He hadn't lied. He wanted her, all right. When at last she raised her head, her breathing was coming in short spurts.

"Ready to do something about it?"

"Garth—"

"Come here," he said, his voice raspy, almost unrecognizable.

Tiffany couldn't move. She could only remain where she was and listen as the rain slashed against the windowpanes, rattling them. Thunder boomed, and lightning danced across the sky.

She flinched, then shivered.

"Don't be afraid." Garth was standing in front of her now, but still not touching her. "The storm will soon pass."

"It's not the storm I'm afraid of." Her voice quivered.

"I know. I feel the same way." He locked a strand of hair behind her ear before leaning over and lightly brushing her lips with the tip of his tongue.

The contact was like an electric current. Her pulse jumped, and she felt as if she'd been stabbed in her lower belly. She reached out and clung to him, so as not to crumple in a heap on the floor.

He nuzzled her neck, then licked it. "You taste so good."

"Kiss me," she whispered achingly, turning her face to meet lips that sank onto hers with a fierce intensity that seemed to suck everything out of her and into him.

He pulled his mouth off hers just long enough to mutter, "You've got on too damn many clothes."

It didn't take him long to remedy that, especially as she didn't raise any protest when, in record time, he discarded her T-shirt, shorts and underwear.

Once she was as naked as he was, she heard his breath catch as he stood back a ways and ran his eyes over her. "You're more beautiful than I ever imagined."

"You probably say that to all your women."

His eyes burned into hers. "There are no other women."

"I—"

"Don't. Just know that I want you and no one else. Just you," Garth repeated, his mouth surrounding a nipple and sucking on it.

"Oh, Garth." Tiffany jammed her fingers in his hair and gave in to the sensations that rocked through her, especially when he cupped his hands around her buttocks, crushing her against his hardness.

"Please," she whispered urgently. "Now. I want you now."

He lifted her, carried her into the dimly lighted bedroom and laid her on the bed. She could see him, see every emotion that flickered across his face.

"I want you, too," he echoed, his voice sounding

thick, as though he'd had too much to drink. "I want you more than I've ever wanted anyone."

He kissed her then, hard and deep. When the kiss ended, he lowered his head and trailed his tongue down her stomach, not even stopping when he reached the curls at the apex of her thighs.

Moaning, she clutched his head and gave in to the waves of pleasure that pounded her body. "Enough!" she finally cried, tugging at him.

Instead of covering her body with his, he rolled off the bed, turned and gently pulled her to the edge of the mattress, where he spread her legs.

Her eyes widened. "What—?"

"It's all right. I want to watch you. I want to watch the expression on your face."

"Garth, please!" she wailed, his provocative words setting her on fire.

Without taking his eyes off her, he bent forward, then thrust his hardness into her moist softness.

"Ohhh," she gasped, feeling him move—in and out, slow, then fast. "Stop teasing me!"

As if he sensed her readiness, he covered both her breasts with his big hands and upped the pace.

Only after they both cried out simultaneously did he collapse on top of her. Then, with him still inside her, he rolled them onto their sides, where they faced each other.

"Did I hurt you?" he asked, when their breathing had settled somewhat.

"No."

"I was afraid I had."

"Why?"

"You were...are so small."

"And you're so big."

He chuckled, brushing her damp hair away from her face. "Whatever. All I know is that it was perfect. Your body's perfect."

"So is yours."

"Have you had many men?"

She didn't know why she answered so personal a question, but she did. "I've only had two affairs. Neither one lasted very long, although I came close to getting married the second time."

"What stopped you?"

"He was a lush, but a master at hiding it."

"Apparently neither one knew a good thing when he had it."

"That's a nice thing to say."

"I meant it."

"What about you?"

"Let's just say I've known my share of women and leave it at that."

Before she could protest, he kissed her, which in turn made her realize that he was hard again.

"I can't get enough of you."

"I'm not complaining," she whispered, even as he turned onto his back, taking her with him.

"Now it's your turn." His eyes smoldered. "To ride me, that is."

She didn't complain about that, either.

"Mmm...what time is it?"

Tiffany's eyes popped open, and she sat straight up in the bed and peered down at a heavy-lidded Garth. It hit her then, like an avalanche, what had happened between them. Although her mind struggled to come to terms with the latest turn of events, she wasn't sorry. She had enjoyed every breathless moment he was inside her, making her climax over and over, until she was drained.

"On second thought, who gives a damn what time it is? I don't."

Having said that, he reached up and pulled her down to him and kissed her soundly. "Good morning."

"Good morning," she echoed, nestling closer.

"Was it good for you?"

Tiffany nodded. "The best."

"Ditto."

For a while they were both quiet.

Finally Garth asked, "So tell me why you want to own your own shop."

"It's simple, really. I like pretty things."

He braced his palm on one side of his head and peered down at her. "Is that the only reason?"

"No, but it ranks right up there at the top."

"So things are important to you?"

Tiffany listened for the censure in his voice, but if it was there, he kept it well hidden. "Damn straight they are."

He smiled. "Sounds like I just stepped on a couple of toes."

"Not mine, my grandmother's."

"What does she have to do with it?"

"A lot, actually." This time Tiffany smiled, a sweet smile. "She reared me after my parents died in a mobile-home fire."

"I'm sorry. Where were you?"

"At Mimi's—that's what I called her." Tiffany paused and took a deep breath. Recalling those memories was synonymous with rubbing the scab off an old wound.

"I take it she's dead?"

"Right, and I still miss her, though she didn't have anything to give me except lots of love. My parents didn't have anything to leave me. My daddy was a carpenter and a drunk. My mother was a housewife with no outside skills. And Mimi was too crippled with arthritis."

"How did you make it financially?"

"Mimi's pension. Then, after school, I'd come home and iron women's clothes for money."

"That couldn't have been much of a life for a kid." His tone was gently sober.

Tiffany shrugged. "It wasn't all that bad, but fingering all those beautiful things made me vow to someday have them for my own."

He stroked her cheek. "I guess that leaves me out."

"Are you by chance asking in?"

The room turned into a sudden hotbed of tension.

"No," he said, averting his gaze.

Tiffany ignored the tiny pain that jabbed her heart. What had she expected? Their night together had been a sexual romp, nothing else, certainly not a lifetime commitment. Still, she was disappointed with his answer, and she hated herself for that.

"So?" she asked, determined to mask her pain with class.

"So, what?"

"So what about you? Do you have a family?"

Although he hesitated, he said, "When I was ten years old, my dad was killed in an automobile accident. Two years later, my mom remarried and had two other children."

"So how did it work out with your stepdad?"

"Great. He's a fine man."

"So what do you do for a living? As in details."

"Mind if I take a rain check on this conversation?"

Tiffany was caught so off guard by his refusal to confide in her that it robbed her of a suitable comeback. All she could do was open and close her mouth, all the while thinking how foolish she must look.

"I promise I'll tell you later." He smiled, kissed her on the tip of the nose, then took her hand and pulled her to her knees. "Come on, I'll race you to the shower."

She could forgive him anything when he smiled like that. "You're on."

A while later, after they had washed each other, then made love under the running water, Tiffany climbed out of the shower, leaving him behind to rinse off.

That wasn't all he was doing. He was singing. She smiled, then hollered, "I know you're not a musician."

He stuck his head around the curtain. "Are you saying I can't sing?"

"That's right. Actually, you sound like you're in pain."

"I'll make you pay for that."

"I'll count on it."

He chuckled before disappearing back behind the curtain, where he wasted no time in beginning his concert again.

Rolling her eyes, Tiffany walked into the bedroom, dressed in her T-shirt and shorts, and was halfway to the kitchen when she heard the knock on the door.

She paused, her brows forming a frown. Should she answer it? After all, this wasn't her place. Then, deciding it didn't matter, that it was no big deal, she crossed to the door and opened it.

Tiffany had no idea who she was expecting, but the visitor wasn't anyone she knew. A woman stood on the porch, one of the most gorgeous creatures she'd ever seen. She was tall and willowy, with black hair that caressed shoulders that were covered in a well-fitting suit.

But it was her bold facial features and petulant lower lip that singled her out, that were her trump cards. For what seemed an interminable length of time, Tiffany was too taken aback to speak.

Meanwhile, the dark-haired beauty was looking Tiffany up and down as if she were no more important than a speck of lint that needed to be brushed aside. "Who the hell are you?" she demanded.

"Maybe I'd like an answer to that same question." Tiffany's tone was cold.

The woman gave Tiffany a nasty smile. "No problem. I'm Darlene Dixon, Garth's wife."

Ten

If the occasion called for it, Garth felt sure, he could have whipped a bear with a switch. Making love did wonders for both the mind and the body. Hell, he couldn't remember when he'd felt better, not even before he suffered his scare.

He was in a hurry to get out of the shower, yet he wasn't. The water hitting his body had the same effect as acupuncture—hot needles pricking his skin, reversing pain into pleasure.

As good as that was, he had something better waiting for him outside the shower—Tiffany. He smiled and belted out another high note on the pop song he was singing. He paused for a second, half expecting to see Tiffany pop her head around the curtain, once more making fun of his inability to carry a tune.

When she didn't appear, he started singing again, his thoughts turning to their lovemaking and its aftermath.

PLAY "LUCKY HE
AND GET . . .

★ **Exciting Silhouette Desire® novel**

★ **PLUS a Lovely Simulated Pearl**

THEN CONTINUE
LUCKY STREAK W
SWEETHEART OF

1. Play Lucky Hearts as instructed o

2. Send back this card and you'll rec
   Desire® novels. These books have
   each, but they are yours to keep a

3. There's no catch. You're under no
   We charge nothing — ZERO —
   And you don't have to make any
   purchases — not even one!

4. The fact is thousands of readers e
   from the Silhouette Reader Servic
   of home delivery…they like getti
   before they're available in stores…
   prices!

5. We hope that after receiving your
   remain a subscriber. But the choi
   or cancel, anytime at all! So why
   invitation, with no risk of any ki

She didn't know he'd awakened during the night and watched her.

He had drunk in the beauty of the thick lashes that fanned against her cheek, her slightly parted lips, the honey-colored hair spread over the pillow and the rise and fall of her bare breasts.

Watching her, of course, had only aroused him all over again. But he hadn't disturbed her. He'd been deriving too much satisfaction from simply looking at her, something he'd never done before.

Then, in the moment after she first awakened, he'd been privy to another pleasurable first, only that first had scared him. He'd seen something odd flash in her eyes, a vulnerable sensuality that reached deep in his gut and squeezed.

He hadn't wanted to feel that way then, and he didn't want to now. She was great in bed; her timidity was refreshing. In fact, he'd never had better sex. Still, in a nutshell, their lives were on a collision course. He didn't give a damn about money, per se. It was the challenge he craved. If making money was the end result, then so be it.

Tiffany, on the other hand, was smitten with the almighty dollar, like his ex-wife. At least Tiffany had admitted that up front, making no bones about it.

Well, he'd been down that primrose path before, and he never intended to repeat the trip. But he also knew that he couldn't *not* see Tiffany again, regardless of how materialistic she was. While he was here, she was his best medicine.

Deciding he was going to turn into a prune if he didn't get out and dry off, Garth turned off the shower and stepped out. He listened for sounds of Tiffany coming from the kitchen and tested the air for the smell of coffee. Neither one was forthcoming.

He wrapped a towel around his waist and walked into the small living room, his destination the kitchen. He never made it.

"Was she as good in bed as me?"

The recognition of that familiar voice coming out of nowhere brought him to a frozen standstill. He felt as though someone had stuck a knife in his unguarded gut. Squinting, he stared at the elegantly dressed woman sitting in a chair that looked as if it had come from Goodwill. He almost laughed at the irony of it all. But there was nothing funny about the situation.

After a stunned moment, Garth found his voice. "What the hell are you doing here?"

"For shame, darling," she said in a cooing tone. "That's no way to talk to your wife."

"Ex." Garth's tone was full of venom.

Darlene shrugged. "A mere technicality."

Tiffany! Where was she? A sick feeling washed through him. He knew where she was. She was gone.

"I know what you're thinking, sweetheart. You never could hide anything from me. And you're right, your lady friend ran like a scalded cat."

"What did you tell her, dammit?"

Darlene pulled a cigarette out of her Gucci purse, a purse bought with his money, and lighted it.

"Put that damn thing out."

She merely shrugged again, tapped the end of it with a long fingernail painted the color of blood, then put it out. He'd never touched this woman in a violent way, not even in their worst moments. But again he felt he could do her bodily harm and not bat an eye.

That thought made him sicker.

"What did you tell her?" he repeated.

Apparently Darlene picked up on the cold steel in his voice. She turned a tad paler, and he saw a flicker of fear in her eyes. Still, when she spoke, there was defiance in her tone. "I told her I was your wife."

"You bitch."

Darlene laughed. "Are you in love with her?"

This time *he* laughed, but without humor. "You haven't changed. But then, I guess you never will. You're beautiful, you're greedy, and you have no soul."

"Takes one to know one." She spit the words at him.

"That's right, and that ain't gonna change."

Darlene's hard features softened suddenly, and her voice turned cooing again. "I didn't come here to fight with you."

"I know why you came. Money. You want more money."

Her eyes tracked his partially nude body, and she swallowed. "Would you believe me if I told you I came to see you? That I still want you?"

"People in hell want ice water, too, and they never get it."

The softness fled from her face. She jumped up out of the chair and glared at him, two red blotches appearing on her cheekbones.

"You had your chance, and you blew it. It's over, Darlene. You're going to have to accept that, because I've had it with your little games. Your showing up here is the straw that broke the camel's back. If you can't handle your life, then I suggest you take some of the money you're getting from me and see a shrink."

"How dare you talk to me like that!"

"Save it," he said in a bored voice. "Besides, we've played this record so many times that it's broken."

The record had actually started with the whining and the relentless phone calls immediately after he told her to pack her bags and get out, having caught her in bed with another man.

It was in that time frame that Garth had realized he'd married a money-crazed whore who cared only for his money and nothing for him. But more than that, she'd killed something vital in him—his trust.

He'd found out all too soon that he'd been living in a fool's paradise. He'd actually hoped for wonderful old-fashioned things from their marriage, such as love, honesty, faithfulness, and even children.

None of his dreams had come anywhere near panning out. Eventually he'd learned to live with the cold, hard fact that he'd made the biggest mistake of his life. What he hadn't been able to live with was her refusal to let him go.

Those phone calls hadn't let up. Each time, she'd begged him to take her back. When the begging didn't work, she'd hurled insults at him, followed by more pleas.

When he refused to answer his phone at home or take her calls at the office, she'd resorted to showing up on his doorstep. Only after he had his heart problem had she slacked off, and he'd figured it was just a brief reprieve.

Her presence here had proved gut instinct right again. He felt nothing for her. It was as if she'd never been a part of his life. Hell, she could move into a house next door to him, parade around naked in her yard, and it wouldn't have any effect on him. Garth suddenly switched his thoughts back to Tiffany and cursed inwardly. What was she thinking? He couldn't begin to dwell on that now, or he wouldn't have enough wherewithal to get rid of Darlene, this time for good. That was his top priority.

"Actually, I came here to tell you I'm getting married," she said, breaking into the long and uncomfortable silence.

His initial reaction was shock, followed by the urge to laugh. His second was to say how he pitied the poor bastard who was taking her on. His third was to admit that God had apparently not deserted him.

He kept those thoughts bottled inside and said, with as much sincerity as he could muster, "I wish you the best of luck."

She didn't miss the cool lack of interest in his voice, and her body seemed to shrink inside itself. Tears formed in her eyes, the only sincere tears he'd ever seen there.

"Goodbye, Garth. I won't bother you anymore."

When the door slammed behind her, he clutched at his chest, not in pain, but in jubilation. Free at last, he thought, turning and walking to the window, where he watched her Mercedes disappear.

Suddenly he craved a drink, only not to celebrate his freedom from Darlene, but to give him the courage to go after Tiffany.

He lifted the bottle and found that he couldn't pour the liquid into a glass. His hands, usually as steady as a rock, were shaking. Finally he managed to get down a healthy sip. What better anesthetic to halt a brain racing like a charged-up engine?

He poured another drink, then slammed down the glass. At least the rain had stopped, which was a good omen. He smiled a genuine smile, making his way into the bedroom, where he got dressed.

Once he explained the situation to Tiffany, she would

understand. First, though, he would give her time to cool off. Then he would make his move. Everything would be all right.

Meanwhile, he would clean this place up. Whistling, he made his way back into the kitchen and grabbed a broom.

Married!

Tiffany had plotted Garth's demise in every conceivable way possible. The sad part about it was that she wouldn't get the chance to turn any of them into reality, because she didn't plan to see Garth Dixon ever again.

Still, reaching that conclusion hadn't let her off the hook. She had made love to a married man, a man who hadn't used any protection. God! She'd done some dumb things in her thirty years, but that was one of the dumbest.

What if she was pregnant?

No! She wouldn't think about that. She couldn't and still keep her sanity. Instead she had to get hold of herself and regroup. What was done was done; she couldn't change it. Yet she still couldn't stop beating up on herself.

It had been two hours since she'd made love to Garth, since she'd given him carte blanche over her body. Suddenly Tiffany felt dizzy, and she caught hold of the edge of the kitchen table until the room settled once again.

The thought of him touching another woman the way he'd touched her made her physically ill. Yet she knew it to be the unvarnished truth. He'd touched his *wife* that way. Tiffany grabbed her stomach and thought she was about to lose the cup of coffee she'd just drunk. To stave off the nausea, she took deep breaths.

She shouldn't have been surprised. She should have

known that someone like Garth Dixon hadn't escaped marriage. The fact that he'd refused to confide in her should have been the first clue.

Fool!

She was that and more. But when she saw him naked, all rational thought had deserted her. Having him make love to her had been all that mattered. She'd never experienced such overwhelming heat, never felt such an ache for a man in her life. When he so obviously returned those feelings, she hadn't been able to resist.

So what now? she asked herself. She couldn't keep up this vicious cycle, replaying those events. Maybe she should go after Taylor. With the little girl in the house, she would be forced to focus on someone other than herself.

Besides, she was lonely. Thank God the rain hadn't returned, which would only have added to her gloom. Looking up, Tiffany stared out the window into the sunshine, then farther off, to the mountains, seeking a solace that wouldn't come.

Damn, but she was hurting.

The phone rang, and her heart skipped a beat. What if it was Garth? Dream on, she thought, a smirk rearranging her lips. He wasn't about to call her. But then, maybe he would; men who ran around on their wives had more gall than a government mule.

On second thought, she hoped it *was* Garth. She would love to give him a verbal flogging. It wouldn't change anything, except to make her feel better, which would be a start on the healing process.

When she said hello, the person responding was definitely not Garth. It was her old boss, Hazel. That in itself was a shock, though of a different kind.

"Am I calling at a bad time?" the other woman asked.

Tiffany smothered a sigh. "No, actually it's a good time." If ever she'd needed a distraction, it was now. Even if it was the witch from hell.

"Good, because we have a lot to talk about."

Tiffany's eyebrows shot up. She couldn't believe what she was hearing. She didn't know when they had *ever* had anything to talk about, much less a lot.

"How did you track me down?"

Hazel chuckled. "You know me. I'm relentless."

That was true enough. "What's up?"

"How much longer are you planning to be there?"

"What's the matter? Have you found something else to blame me for?"

"No, not at all."

"Hazel, just get to the point, okay? It's not as if you and I parted on a friendly basis."

Although her ex-boss didn't respond with similar bluntness, Tiffany knew she would have liked to. That was one reason why they couldn't work together; they were too much alike.

"I won't argue that point, only…"

"Only what?" Tiffany pressed her, if for no other reason than to end this conversation, seeing as it was going nowhere.

"I'm retiring, and I've recommended you for my job." Hazel paused. "Are you interested?"

Eleven

"**H**ow are you?"

Tiffany forced a smile. "I'm supposed to be asking you that. After all, you're the one in the hospital bed, not me."

Bridget's forehead wrinkled. "Well, if you'll pardon me for saying it, you should be in the one next to me."

"Do I look that bad?"

"Worse."

They both giggled; Tiffany had felt the need to see her friend. She had hoped this unplanned visit would take her mind off Garth. Her ploy had worked.

Then she turned serious as she stared at Bridget, who she was relieved to see looked much improved and well on her way to a full recovery. In both cases, that would be a blessing, especially for her. The sooner she got out of Pennington, and away from Garth, the sooner she could look herself in the mirror once again. Maybe.

"Seriously, what's up?" Bridget asked.

"Where's Jeremiah?"

"Oh, no, you don't. You're not going to get by with changing the subject."

"I wasn't trying to, not really. While I was here, I just wanted to say hi to your hubby."

"Fine, that's not a problem. He's having a hamburger in the cafeteria. I expect him back shortly."

Tiffany glanced at her watch. "Gosh, it *is* that time. Usually my stomach tells me when it's lunchtime."

"Something's obviously killed your appetite. So let's have it. What's going on?" Bridget smiled, which seemed to kick the freckles across her nose front and center. "Surely my daughter's being gone isn't responsible for your funk." Her smile had turned mischievous, and she cocked her head to one side.

"Believe it or not, I do miss her. That house is like a tomb without her."

"She's a live wire, all right." Bridget's scrutiny became more intense. "So?"

Tiffany gave her a cross look. "God, you're relentless. I can see you still haven't lost that courtroom edge."

Bridget smiled again. "That's what Jeremiah says. But he doesn't have any room to talk. He's just as bad. His head's harder than a brick. I've tried my best to get him to go home for just a few hours, for heaven's sake, but he refuses." Bridget rolled her eyes. "Men!"

You've got that right, Tiffany thought, that awful feeling once more invading the pit of her stomach. "Hell's bells, leave him alone," she said. "You ought to be glad he wants to stay with you. Most men would've high-tailed it out of here the first chance they got. You're lucky, so count your blessings."

"You're sure on a toot."

Tiffany's mouth curved down; then she gave Bridget a sheepish smile. "Guess I am at that."

"So what's the bottom line here? Are you trying to find the courage to tell me you need to leave? Is that what's bothering you?"

"Yes and no."

"I understand perfectly."

Tiffany grinned. "I knew you would."

"If I was able, I'd smack you."

"I need it."

"If you don't tell me what's going on, I'm—"

"Okay, you've made your point. I do need to talk."

"About what?"

Tiffany's tone was tinged with both suspicion and curiosity. "For one thing, my old boss, Hazel, called."

"The witch? You're kidding?"

"Nope." Tiffany grinned. "She's leaving, and she recommended me as her replacement."

"What on earth came over her?"

"The only thing I can think of is she got laid."

Bridget laughed. "Well, that's been known to cure a lot of ills."

"Not in my case," Tiffany muttered, then regretted having opened her mouth and putting her foot in it.

"What did you say?"

"Nothing. Forget it."

"It isn't nothing, and we won't forget it." Bridget's tone brooked no argument. "I'm tired of playing this pull-it-out-of-me game. Sounds to me like you got some yourself."

In spite of her determination to keep her cool, Tiffany felt her face turn beet red. She hated the fact that Bridget could read her so well. Or maybe she was just wearing her battered heart on her shoulder for everyone to see. "As a matter of fact, I did."

Bridget's jaw dropped. *"You did?"*

"Yes," Tiffany said tightly.

"But who? I mean—" Bridget's voice played out in a sputter, and then her face glowed. "Don't tell me you and—"

"Garth Dixon," Tiffany finished for her.

Bridget blinked, as if she were still trying to make sense out of this latest revelation. Then her lips curved in the barest hint of a smile. "That would be our neighbor, of course?"

"Do you know another Garth Dixon?" Tiffany snapped, knowing that Bridget was teasingly jerking her chain.

Bridget bubbled with laughter. "Wonders never cease."

"It's not funny."

"You made love to the man whose brain you addled. Why, I think that's hilarious."

"Bridget!"

"Okay, okay. But you'll have to forgive me if I don't find that such a catastrophe. I think it's great, actually. After all, you're both over twenty-one and in command of all your faculties."

When Tiffany remained silent, Bridget went on. "So how did the two of you—"

"It's a long story," Tiffany said, interrupting her, wishing now that she'd never opened her mouth. It was so humiliating, since the incident didn't have a happy ending.

Still, she had to confide in someone, and who better than her best friend, if for no other reason than to absolve her conscience and try to sort out what she'd done?

"I have nothing else to do but listen," Bridget said into the growing silence.

"What about physical therapy?"

"You're the one who's going to need physical therapy if you don't tell me what the hell's going on."

"All right, you win," Tiffany said.

After she finished her story—leaving out the sexual details, of course—Bridget sat still, as if dumbfounded. Then she finally said, "You mean…" Again she faltered.

"Yep. He's married. I slept with a married man."

"Well, it's not the end of the world, you know."

"That's easy for you to say."

"As long as you used protection, then it's okay."

"So when are you planning on getting out of this hole?"

Bridget wiggled upward, into a straighter position. "There you go again. You're *not* changing the subject this time, either."

"Look…"

"He *did* use protection, right?"

"Wrong," Tiffany said in a small voice, at the same time averting her gaze.

"Oh, Tiff!" Bridget wailed.

Tiffany swung back around to stare at her friend. "I know. Pretty dumb, huh?"

"I can't judge. I've been there myself. You'll just have to put it behind you and pray that your mistake doesn't cost you big-time."

"I wish it were that easy."

"It is. Just go back to Houston and take that job. Now."

"What about Taylor?"

"I'm sure Lilah can keep her until I get out."

"No, that wasn't the deal, and I'm not reneging on my word."

The room fell quiet for another minute. Then Bridget said, in a tentative tone, "Did his...wife say anything?"

"Nope. She just identified herself, and I got the hell out of there."

"I take it you haven't seen or talked to Garth since then."

"No, and I don't intend to. Not if I can help it, that is."

"What a slimy jerk."

Tiffany laughed a humorless laugh. "You're being kind."

"I can imagine what you've called him."

"No, you can't."

Bridget smiled. "Hey, it's not the end of the world. What's done is done. Just think of it as one of those fluky, crazy things that happen to us once in a lifetime, then chalk it up to experience."

"Chalk what up to experience?"

Neither one of them had heard Jeremiah when he walked into the room. His smiling face no longer had the gaunt, pinched look that had been there the last time Tiffany saw him. That alone told her that Bridget was indeed on the road to recovery, which tempered some of her own misery.

"Not a thing, darling," Bridget said, grinning. "Just woman talk."

"Figures." He smiled at Tiffany. "So, how are things?"

"Hunky-dory," Tiffany lied.

"I bet so, especially now that you're rid of the little tornado around the house."

"I actually miss that little tornado. It's lonely without her."

Jeremiah reached for his wife's outstretched hand. "So do we, but it won't be much longer until we're back home and our family's together again."

"When that happens," Tiffany said, "we'll throw a party."

"You betcha." Then, changing the subject, Jeremiah asked, "So, is Garth still looking after things, or have you got him running scared?" His lips twitched, and he grinned.

Tiffany forced a smile of her own, while Bridget's eyes widened. "Not to worry. Everything's under control."

"That's a relief."

"Guess I'd best be going." Tiffany threw Bridget an almost desperate look.

Bridget motioned for her to come to the bed. "Not until you give me another hug."

Tiffany did just that, then straightened.

"Don't go on my account," Jeremiah said. "Just pretend I'm not here."

"I don't think so, sweetheart," Bridget said with humorous sarcasm.

"I'll see you two later, okay?" Tiffany said, then left.

A short time later, a grim-faced Tiffany pulled up in front of the ranch house. She had just stepped inside and dumped her purse on the couch when the phone rang. She considered not answering it.

Her desire to confront Garth had passed. She didn't want to talk to anyone else, either. Still, she found herself dashing in that direction and lifting the receiver.

"Tiffany?"

Her worst fears had turned into reality. "I don't have anything to say—"

"Don't hang up! Please."

It wasn't so much what Garth said as the way he said it that made her hesitate. "You have your nerve, you bastard. Give me one good reason why I shouldn't slam this receiver down in your ear."

"Taylor."

Tiffany's heart lurched. "What about Taylor? Has something happened to her?"

"Yes, but—"

"But *what?*" Her voice was thin.

"Calm down and let me finish. She's had an accident. She cut her hand, but she's going to be all right."

"Where is she?"

"In the hospital. Lilah and I are here with her."

"I'm on my way."

Tiffany slammed down the phone and ran out the door, back to her car. Only after she was on the highway did she ask herself how the hell Garth had become involved. She guessed she would find out soon enough.

Damn! She pounded the steering wheel and fought back tears. It was bad enough that something had happened to Taylor, but to have to face Garth again so soon was almost as bad.

"You're a real trouper, you know that?"

Despite Garth's assurance, Taylor's lower lip trembled slightly. "It hurts."

"'Course it does," Lilah said, taking Taylor's hand in hers.

Tiffany realized that they didn't know she was there. The curtain to Taylor's cubbyhole in the emergency facility was open. Tiffany stood on the threshold and quickly assessed the situation. The child was sitting upright on a gurney, her face showing signs of dried tears, Lilah on one side and Garth on the other.

Tiffany tried to force her eyes to stay solely on Lilah and Taylor, but she couldn't. They landed on Garth. As usual, he had on what she'd come to identify as his favorite mode of dress: worn jeans that were slightly baggy on his lean hips and long legs, a leather belt, and a blue short-sleeved shirt that exposed his tanned skin.

It wasn't how he looked, though he was as sexy and attractive as ever—and did her body ever react, going into meltdown—but it was the way he was looking at Taylor, the gentle expression in his eyes, that held her motionless.

Apparently Taylor sensed it, as well, for she held out her arms to Garth and said, "Hold me, then maybe it won't hurt so much."

Tears welled up in Tiffany's eyes, and she wanted to cry out to Taylor that *she* would hold her, but the tears had her throat clogged.

"How 'bout if I sit on the bed beside you and put my arms around you?" Before Taylor could respond, Garth did just that. "The doctor might not like it if you got out of bed."

Taylor nestled in the crook of his arm, seemingly perfectly content.

What a complete contradiction this man was, Tiffany thought. She would never in a million years have pegged him for someone who liked children. But then, for all she knew, he had children of his own.

After all, he *was* married. Another sharp pang hit her.

"Tiffany!" Lilah said. "How long have you been standing there?"

Tiffany shifted her eyes to Taylor, though she answered Lilah. ''Not long. What happened?''

''Me and Mama Lilah were cuttin' peaches and my knife slipped,'' Taylor said, her lower lip beginning to quiver again.

Tiffany went to her side, and when she did, Garth got up. She took his place, careful not to look at him. Still, she felt his gaze on her.

''I'm so sorry.''

''Me too,'' Taylor said, returning her hug.

Tiffany examined the bandaged wound on Taylor's left index finger, then peered over at Lilah. ''Is everything under control?''

''It is now,'' Lilah said, in a rather unsteady voice. ''Thanks to Garth, that is.''

''Oh?'' Tiffany said. ''How did…Garth get in on it?''

''I was at your place,'' he said from behind, ''and I heard the phone ring. I answered it, and the rest is history, as they say.''

''I see,'' Tiffany responded, still not looking at him. ''So when can I take her home?''

''They just gave her a tetanus shot,'' Lilah said. ''We're waiting to make sure she doesn't have a reaction. Then she'll be free to go.'' She paused. ''I'd like to take her back home with me, if you don't mind.''

Tiffany frowned as she turned to Taylor. ''It's up to you, honey.''

''I guess I should stay with Mama Lilah, 'cause my friend next door's having a birthday party tomorrow.''

''All right, puddin'.'' Tiffany caressed her cheek. ''I—''

She never got to finish her sentence, because a tall, gray-headed man walked in, settling his smiling eyes on the child. ''Well, young lady, you appear to be okay.

Your family can take you home now.'' He turned to Lilah. "I'll want to see her again in a couple of days."

"I'll have her here."

"Up you go, honey," Garth said, lifting her into his arms.

Moments later, Tiffany stood by while Lilah climbed behind the wheel and Garth sat Taylor beside her. Their goodbyes were said, but she still refused to acknowledge Garth. She spotted her own car close by and headed toward it.

"Tiffany, wait up."

She hated herself for stopping, and even more for turning around.

"We have to talk," he said, his eyes almost pleading.

"I don't think so."

"Well, I do. I can explain."

"I just bet you can."

Ignoring her bitterness, he said, "But not here."

"Save your breath, on me at least. If there's any explaining to do it should be to your wife. Don't you think?"

"Dammit," he snapped, his gaze swinging to the other people in the busy parking lot. Then, lowering his voice, he went on, "She's not—"

"Stop it! I'm not interested in anything you have to say."

His face lost its color, and he snapped his mouth shut as she turned her back on him. But she hadn't missed the look in his eyes. Despite the hot, glaring sun, a chill passed through her.

Something told her that she hadn't heard the last of this, that he *would* get his day in court.

Twelve

———

"How 'bout some more coffee?"

Tiffany smiled at Irma, then held out her cup. "Thanks, but you don't have to wait on me, you know."

"Why not? For the moment, you're the only one here."

"That's only because it's early-thirty." Tiffany took a sip of the hot liquid and looked at her watch. "I can't believe I got up at the crack of dawn."

Irma smiled, which filled out her tiny face a bit. "I'm glad you did. I love having special friends stop by before the hustle and bustle starts."

Tiffany reached out and squeezed her hand. "You make everyone feel special, even a stranger like me."

"Nonsense. You're no stranger. Actually, I don't guess I've ever met a stranger."

Tiffany laughed, then fell silent.

Irma gave her an odd look, then said, "Something's bothering you, isn't it?"

"How did you know?"

"Remember, I'm an old lady who's been around the mulberry bush a time or two. Besides, it's obvious you haven't been getting any sleep. Your eyes look like someone used you for a punching bag."

"Ouch!" Tiffany responded with mock humor.

"Sorry, but it's the truth." Irma softened her bluntness with a sympathetic smile.

Tiffany sighed but still didn't say anything, all the while trying to collect her thoughts. "You're right, I haven't been sleeping."

"Is it Taylor and the accident?"

"I'm sure that figures into it, although she's all right now."

"So are you ready to go home? Is that it?"

"Yes and no." Tiffany gave her a wan smile. "I've just had a really good job offer. Nothing I want permanently, however," she added. "Still, I can't afford not to give it some serious thought."

"And have you?"

"Not much."

Irma chuckled. "Then you must not want it very badly."

"I'm not sure I know *what* I want."

"Could that have something to do with Garth Dixon?"

Irma's quietly spoken question came out of nowhere, and hit Tiffany like a karate chop from behind. If she hadn't been sitting, her legs would have buckled, sending her down for the count.

"What on earth made you ask that?"

Irma chuckled again. "I may be old, child, but I'm not blind."

"So what are you saying?" Tiffany tried to keep her expression blank, but she knew she'd failed. She'd never been good at hiding her feelings. If she was glad, everyone knew it; if she was unhappy, everyone knew that, too.

"Remember I saw the way you two looked at one another in the store."

"That's hogwash," Tiffany said, a rush of color invading her cheeks.

"Is it? I don't think so."

Tiffany turned away, mortified that her secret was apparently no secret after all. She would have to be careful, or the whole world would know.

"Have you seen him since Taylor cut her hand?"

Tiffany raised her eyebrows. "How did you know he was involved?"

"In this town, honey, nothing is secret or sacred."

"I guess that's so foreign to me I can't quite comprehend it. In Houston, your neighbors don't give a damn what you do."

"Well, living in a blink-and-you-miss-it kind of town definitely has its minuses." Irma paused to sip her coffee. "But it also has its pluses—neighbors see about neighbors." She paused again. "And I haven't seen Garth in several days."

"So?" Tiffany asked, with as much nonchalance as she could muster. Dammit, she didn't want to think about Garth or talk about him. Yet she couldn't seem to stop doing either, especially with Irma continually stirring that hornet's nest.

She should take Bridget up on her offer to let Taylor remain with Lilah. Then she could return to Houston, where she belonged. Once there, she could take that job on a short-term basis, which would be the sane and wise thing to do.

Then why the hell didn't she? Why was she still here, in this town, talking about the man who'd made a fool out of her? She had to let her hot emotions stop overruling her sound judgment.

Still, all was not lost. She'd been proud of the way she handled the situation at the emergency room the day after she slept with Garth. It hadn't been easy; in fact, it had been hell, for despite his underhanded betrayal, the power remained with him. He had only to come near her and her body heat shot up.

Time and distance would temper that. Let him have his wife. From what she could tell, they deserved one another.

"Tiffany, are you all right?" Irma asked.

"I'm fine," she fibbed, forcing a smile to reinforce the lie.

"Look, I don't know what's going on between you two, and I don't want to—unless you want me to. Even so, I'm concerned about Garth, especially since he never misses coming to the store." She pinched the bridge of her nose, as though warding off a headache. "It's not a good sign, him with that bad heart, and alone in that cabin."

Tiffany made an unladylike noise. "That's where you're wrong."

"What do you mean?"

"He isn't alone. At least, he wasn't."

"You mean someone's with him?"

"Yeah, his wife."

Irma blinked, then something flickered in her eyes that caught Tiffany's attention. "What?"

"Are you saying that pretty, dark-haired lady is his wife?"

"Yep. Only how did you know what she looked like?"

"She stopped here for gas on her way out of town." Irma smiled. "And I'd say she was anything but happy, if that frown on her face was anything to judge by. So if Garth's her husband, then there's obviously trouble in paradise."

On hearing that his wife had left the cabin, Tiffany's breathing turned jerky before finally settling back to normal. "That's no skin off my back. I couldn't care less."

"Then you won't mind doing me a favor and checking on him."

"I don't—"

"While you're at it, give him this loaf of homemade bread." Irma got up and walked over to the counter where she grabbed a package. "It's sweet-potato bread—his favorite."

"I never said I'd do that favor."

"Well, will you?" Irma asked pointedly.

"No," she said, only to mutter immediately afterward, "Yes."

"Which is it, my dear?" Irma asked in a calm voice, as if this were an ordinary conversation.

Tiffany knew better. There was nothing ordinary about this conversation, or the situation. It was mind-boggling. She couldn't believe she'd let Irma manipulate her. However, the fat lady hadn't sung yet. She could still change her mind, and she wouldn't feel the least bit guilty.

He should be the one who felt guilty. The son of a bitch was married, and he hadn't told her.

"I don't know," Tiffany finally said tersely.

Irma didn't seem to take offense, especially as someone sauntered in the door just then. "Go on, take the
bread. If you decide not to take it to him, I'll understand." She broke off with a wink. "You eat it. You'll
think you died and went to heaven. I promise."

Again Tiffany couldn't contain her smile. Later, back
at the ranch, that smile remained intact. But not for long.
Damn Irma for mentioning Garth in the first place. And
damn her for planting the seed of the thought that something terrible might have happened to him.

He wasn't *her* responsibility. Tiffany's eyes strayed
to the loaf of bread on the table, then glanced away, then
turned back again.

Should she take it to him? As a favor to Irma?

The sun felt good on his bare back. It was actually
therapeutic for his entire body, tranquil. Too bad those
feelings didn't carry over to his mind. It was still raging.

It was all *her* fault. Tiffany had somehow managed to
worm her way inside his head and make him crazy.
Since he met her, he hadn't had a rational thought. What
she'd done was knock him senseless, addle his brain.
That had to be the only logical explanation for what he'd
just done.

Before he wandered down to the orchard, he'd talked
to Jeremiah at the hospital, then to a cattleman Jeremiah
had recommended, having decided to invest in a few
head of cattle.

Now, as he pulled some weeds from around a tree, he
couldn't help but smile. If his cohorts back home could
see him, they wouldn't believe it. Well, he didn't, either.
Hell, he was a corporate man, not a sodbuster, for God's
sake. But it was Tiffany who had planted that seed, the
day they freed the trapped calf.

Since then, the thought had been niggling in the back of his mind, which was insane. And this peach orchard—that had been bugging him, as well. He hated waste, and if something wasn't done soon, this crop would be lost.

Maybe he could deal with the peaches; they required work only once a year. But cattle—their needs were ongoing. Who would tend to them when he left and went back to civilization?

Hell, maybe he just wouldn't budge. Maybe he would just stay here. An expletive crossed his lips.

Tiffany.

Again his churning, irrational thoughts were her fault. If he hadn't made love to her, hadn't tasted her exquisite body, then the nesting bug wouldn't be nibbling around the edges of his mind. Hell, after he got rid of Darlene, he'd sworn never to get emotionally involved with another woman. And he'd held true to that vow—until Tiffany.

He hadn't a clue as to how or why she was different. She just was. Maybe she fascinated him because he couldn't figure out if she was a gold digger or an angel. His brain voted for the former, but his heart voted for the latter, having experienced her magic touch in bed. But at the moment, he didn't give a damn about either.

What he *did* give a damn about was the interminable ache between his legs.

Disgusted, Garth whipped around and headed back toward the cabin. That was when he saw her, as if she had appeared out of nowhere. He broke his stride and came to a halt, thinking that the sunlight, beating down on her blond hair, did indeed make her seem like an angel. The bulge in his jeans grew tighter as he met her halfway.

"You're the last person I expected to see," he said with a grimace.

Tiffany didn't say anything. She was held spellbound by the air of raw manhood he exuded. Would she ever get past that? He was wearing a pair of ragged cutoffs and no shirt. She watched sweat trickle down his face and neck, into the hairs on his chest, which enhanced that raw sexuality. How could he still attract her like this? Married or not, he did. And she hated herself for that.

"Tiffany."

She shook her head as if to clear it, then licked her lips. "My coming here was Irma's idea."

The light in his eyes diminished. "Oh. I see."

"She was worried about you."

"And you weren't?"

"In my place, would you be?"

"It depends on what the other night meant to you."

She was aghast. "You don't have any qualms about rubbing salt in an oozing wound, do you?"

"I'd say you have that same problem. I've tried to explain about Darlene, only you wouldn't listen."

"Tell me why I should. You're the one who lied, who's—"

"I'm not married, Tiffany."

His words, so low and intensely spoken, fell between them with the impact of a shotgun blast. She opened her mouth, and was about to speak when he continued.

"Oh, I *was* married to her, I'll admit that. But not anymore."

"You mean—"

"I mean she's my *ex*-wife, which she failed to tell you."

It was as though a dam had suddenly broken inside Tiffany, sending her emotions cascading in all different directions. She didn't know whether to be jubilant or to run like she'd never run before. "Why would she lie?"

"She was testing the waters."

"She wants you back." Tiffany's tone was as flat as her words.

"People in hell want ice water, too, but they don't get it."

She smiled in spite of herself. "Is that what you told her?"

Garth's gaze never wavered. "Sure did."

"What did she say?"

"You don't wanna know."

"Yes, I do."

"Actually, that's when she told me she was going to marry someone else."

Tiffany gave him an incredulous look. "Just like that?"

"Just like that. But, hey, enough about Darlene. She's history."

"And what am I?" Once the words had passed her lips, Tiffany couldn't believe she'd said them. She felt the color drain from her face.

"The here and now," he said thickly. "Someone I want more than I've wanted anything in my life."

She swallowed against the rising tide of heat. "I'm still not sure what that means."

"Come here," he said in a gruff tone, "and I'll show you."

Thirteen

He didn't know who actually made the first move, but it wasn't important. The only thing that was important was that she hadn't rejected him, that her arms were locked around him as tightly as his were around her. And when his lips took hers, they were moist, pliant and quivering, a combination that sent his heart and his pulse rate skyrocketing.

He couldn't think. His mind went south, and he lost all touch with reality. He could only take the sweetness she was offering and, in doing so, feel his body ignite with a need he couldn't control.

He had to have her. Now!

"Garth," she whispered into his mouth.

Her anxiety, her uncertainty, was apparent in that raspy use of his name. He couldn't reassure her; hell, he couldn't even reassure himself, not when he was so hot, so ready, that he was in pain.

"Feel how much I want you." He ground out the words, anchoring her tighter against him.

It was then that she squirmed, as if trying to get even closer. He couldn't stand that. "If you don't stop that—"

"You'll do what?"

She leaned back then, so that he could see the same heat that was inside him reflected in her eyes.

"I'll take you right here." His voice was guttural.

Those heat-filled eyes widened now, and when she spoke, her voice sounded slightly dazed. "Is that a threat or a promise?"

"Neither. It's a fact."

"Oh, Garth," she said, moving her hands from behind his neck, down his back, until she came to his buttocks. She grabbed each cheek and began to move up, down, around.

"Tiffany!"

After muttering her name in agony, he stepped backward and dragged her with him. Finally his legs bumped against the front of the oversize but tattered chair that was sitting under a huge cottonwood tree.

He eased into it at the same time that he lifted her onto his lap, his hardness pressing against her. She sucked in her breath as his eyes locked on her breasts, breasts that were clearly outlined under her pale yellow T-shirt, especially as that shirt was wet with sweat, making it obvious that she wasn't wearing a bra. Her nipples were turgid and seemed to be begging to escape the confines of the wet fabric.

He groaned out loud, then lowered his head, taking one nipple into his mouth and sucking.

"Yes, yes," she cried softly.

He soon left that nipple and went to the other one.

She cried again, or was it a mewing sound? He couldn't tell, but he didn't care. He cared only about being inside her. With that in mind, he withdrew his mouth and reached frantically for the button of his cutoffs.

She stilled his hand. "Let me."

"Are you sure?" His voice was so hoarse, he didn't even recognize it.

"I'm sure."

He watched as she dropped to her knees between his legs and popped open the button, then unzipped the zipper. She lifted dazed eyes to his.

"Are you sure?" he managed to say through his tight throat.

She nodded, then lowered her head.

"Tiffany, Tiffany, Tiffany," he murmured shortly, while writhing in sweet agony.

Unable to take any more, he grasped her by the shoulders and lifted her to her feet. Seconds later, her clothes were strewn on the ground, and he was easing her down on him.

"Perfect," he whispered, positioning his hands on either side of her hips and moving her back and forth.

"Ohh!"

Her cry was right on target with his, as they both moved together in a shattering climax.

"What are you thinking about?" she asked, shifting slightly, so as to peer down at him.

She was once again in his lap, once again under the same shade tree, in the same chair, but only after they had gone inside, showered and redressed.

Now she had asked him a question he was having trouble answering, because there was so much to think about. He had never been so anxious, yet so tranquil, in his life. Everything about her seemed right for him, but in his gut, he knew she was so wrong. He couldn't bring himself to commit himself to another woman.

It just wasn't in the cards. Yet...

"Aren't you going to answer me?" Tiffany asked. The question was followed by a sigh.

"I was thinking about us."

"Yeah, me too."

"So who's going to confess first?" he asked.

Tiffany didn't quibble. "Do you realize that we haven't used any protection? Not even once?"

He hadn't wanted to face that fact, but now that she'd brought it out in the open, he had no choice. "Yes." His tone was bleak.

"Which is not smart."

"Right."

He wanted to say more, but what more was there to say? If she turned up pregnant... A barrage of sweat broke out on his skin. He would *not* think about that. *Could not* think about that. At least not now, not when she was curled in his lap, with her breasts poking into his chest, and he was fighting off the urge to take her again.

When the silence seemed to grow with the rising breeze, she said, "I should go."

Garth's hold tightened. "No, you shouldn't."

"This is crazy. We both know that. Nothing can come—"

"What's wrong with our making love? We're both adults, and it makes us both feel damn good."

He saw the expression that flickered across her face, and though he wouldn't presume to read her mind, he felt he hadn't given the answer she wanted to hear. But, dammit, that was the best he could do.

"I can't argue with that."

"So next time we'll use protection."

She smiled and thrust her hands into his hair. "Is that all you think about?"

"With you, yes."

Her eyes glittered down at him. "Do you and Darlene have any children?"

Garth felt himself stiffen. He didn't know what he'd been expecting her to say, but it wasn't that. "No, we don't."

"Was that your idea or hers?"

"She didn't want to stretch her body out of its perfect shape."

Tiffany laughed suddenly, which went a long way toward lightening a heavy subject. "That's a new one on me."

"Well, it's the truth."

"What about you? Did you want children? I saw how good you were with Taylor."

"It would've been all right," he admitted, though reluctantly. "But now, I've definitely changed my mind. This world's too sorry to bring kids into. Besides, I have too much going on."

"I'm glad you said that. I'm calling in my rain check."

He winced inwardly. "Which means?" he asked with caution.

"It's your turn to talk about yourself. You've never told me what you did back in Dallas."

"Nothing but boring office work," he lied.

"Boring or not, you still wouldn't have come here if you didn't have a bad heart."

"You're right about that."

"So how *is* your heart?"

Their eyes met and held for a long moment.

"If I make love to you much more, it's going to conk out on me for sure." His lips twitched.

Her eyes glowed with a renewed flare of passion, but when she spoke, her voice was cool. "Which is all the more reason why we shouldn't see each other anymore. One reason among others, of course."

"Hey, I was just teasing," Garth said, panicked at the thought that she might mean what she'd said.

"Were you?"

"Yes, dammit, and you know it. I don't want to stop seeing you." His voice turned husky. "In fact, I'm addicted."

And he was. Still, he didn't know what to do about it.

"I—"

Garth placed her hand on his lap. "Satisfied?"

Color flooded her face even as she removed her hand.

They were quiet for a long moment; then he said, "I'm considering staying here."

"You are?"

She sounded as stunned as he felt. He couldn't believe he had blurted that out. For someone who didn't want his business known, he was sure doing his share of blabbing.

"Permanently?" she asked into the silence.

"As permanent as anything can be in this day and age."

"You know what I mean," she countered, in an exasperated tone.

"I know. It's just that the idea's so new to me that I haven't really come to grips with it myself."

"So what would you do?"

"I've already talked to Jeremiah about buying some cattle."

"After watching you with that calf, I think you should go for it."

"I have a buddy in Dallas who deals in bulls. I'm also thinking about calling him." He paused. "Then there's the peach crop."

Tiffany took her eyes off his and looked toward the rows of fruit-filled trees. "No doubt about it, you certainly have a tiny gold mine there."

"Only I don't have a clue how to go about mining that gold."

"I do."

His mouth parted.

She grinned, then clamped her lips back together, before turning her gaze back on the trees. "Right now, those peaches are just begging to be harvested."

Garth's lips formed a grin before he tugged on a strand of her hair, forcing her eyes back to his. "Now just how would a city girl like you know that?"

She gave him a sharp look, then backed off his lap. "The way you said 'city girl' makes me think you just bit into an apple and found a worm."

He thought she was cracking a joke. On closer observation, however, he realized that humor didn't figure into it. She appeared to be coiled as tight as a rattler about to strike.

"Maybe that's how I feel," he said, with an ease he wasn't feeling.

"I'm not anything like your wife, Garth."

"I didn't say you were."

"Not in so many words, but that's what you meant."

"Look, don't you think you're getting bent out of shape over nothing?"

"Maybe, maybe not. Just because a person wants the things money can buy doesn't mean they're less than human."

Garth tightened his lips into a thin line in order to keep from saying something that he would be sorry for. One minute they were devouring each other's bodies, the next they were duking it out verbally. How had things gone to hell in a handbasket so fast?

"Look, no offense intended, okay? Maybe when it comes to Darlene and her moneygrubbing nature, I do tend to get paranoid."

Tiffany scraped the dirt with a polished toenail, then squinted up at him. "Maybe I overreacted, too."

"Truce?"

"Truce."

"So what did you have in mind?" he asked, fighting the urge to kiss her again. God, she was even sexier when she got mad.

"Come on. I'll show you."

He had no choice but to follow, wondering what the hell was on her mind and what he was getting himself into.

Fourteen

She hadn't meant to say anything. Somehow, though, she couldn't seem to stop opening her mouth and inserting her foot.

Her past was something she didn't care to think or talk about. Already she'd told Garth more than she'd told anyone else, even Bridget. Her friend had no idea just how dismal Tiffany's childhood had been.

"I know something's working in that head of yours," Garth said. "Only I still don't know what."

They had walked to the orchard in silence. The sun was bright, and the temperature ferocious in its intensity. Tiffany paid little attention to either as she glanced up at Garth.

"You're about to find out."

He gave her another uncertain look, accompanied by a half smile. "I'm waiting, and not very patiently, either."

"We're going to harvest these peaches."

"'We' as in 'us'?"

"Yes, and maybe a few farmhands."

"A few farmhands, huh?"

He was teasing her, but she ignored it. "I swore I'd never do this type of labor again," Tiffany said in a faraway voice, her mind having switched back to her childhood days.

"You mean you've actually done this before? Picked peaches, I mean." His tone was incredulous.

"Let's walk through the orchard, okay?"

"Suits me. It's hot as hell here under this bald sunlight."

"Still, it doesn't seem as hot here as it does in Texas," Tiffany said. "Even though the temperature's much higher."

"It's the difference in the humidity."

"That's what they say."

"Although the verdict's still out, I'm thinking I like this climate better." Garth smiled down at her. "What about you?"

"Right now, I vote for Texas."

"That's too bad."

Tiffany thought he sounded genuinely disappointed, but when she looked at him again, his expression was unreadable.

"How did we get off on the weather, anyway?" he asked. "I thought we were talking about peaches."

"We were." Tiffany paused to gather her thoughts. "Remember when I told you I lived with my grandmother, and that I ironed for people after school to supplement her social security check?"

"Of course I do."

"Well, I also worked for our next-door neighbor, who had a farm."

"A peach farm." His words were a flat statement of fact.

She gave him a brief smile. "How'd you guess?"

"I can't imagine," he said, his own lips toying with a smile.

"Old man Hendrix taught me not only how to grow peaches, but how to pick them as well. He also taught me to identify the different varieties."

"Well, I'll be damned."

They had stopped walking and were standing still in the midst of trees weighted down with the delicious-smelling fruit. "Shocked you, haven't I?"

"Again," Garth said, rubbing the top of his head.

"Well, I'm shocked that I told you."

"Why?"

She shrugged. "I don't know."

"It's nothing to be ashamed of, you know."

"I know. Hard work never hurt anyone. Isn't that what they say?" Tiffany inhaled, then was quiet for a moment. "After I stopped working in the orchard, I wouldn't eat a peach for the longest time. And when all that peach potpourri, and hair and body stuff, became popular, I was repulsed."

"And now?"

"I guess I either grew up or got over it. Anyway, all I feel now is a responsibility not to let these beauties go to waste."

"So you're really serious about harvesting them?"

"Not only that, but taking them into Hurricane to market."

"As in selling them?" Again Garth's tone was incredulous.

"Yep." She tried to hide her exasperation at his attitude. "To a grocery store. You have a better idea?"

"Me? Hell, how would I know? I thought maybe I'd ask Irma or Jeremiah what to do with them, if anything."

"Now you don't have to. You *can* use the money, can't you?"

He seemed so taken aback by the mention of money that for a moment she thought she might have offended him. Then a strange look crossed his face, one she couldn't identify. It had been too fleeting.

Suddenly she felt bad. She shouldn't have been so blunt about the money. At best, that was a touchy subject with almost everyone. So what if he didn't have deep pockets or a big bank account? That wasn't anything to her. More to the point, she was sure he didn't like being reminded of the fact that he wasn't successful monetarily.

"Uh, sure I can use the money. I told you I was thinking about buying a few cattle."

Tiffany felt instant relief as she scrutinized him. Apparently he hadn't taken offense. "I'm guessing we can get two truckloads, maybe even more," she said in a businesslike tone.

"You really think it's worth the effort?"

"You bet. It would be terrible for all this to go to waste." Her eyes swept the area.

"I can't say it hasn't bothered me, just not enough to do anything about it."

She turned back to him. "That's because you didn't know what to do. Now, thanks to me, you do. But we'll have to get some help, because I'm sure you shouldn't be doing manual labor, not with your heart."

"You let me be the judge of that."

"Sorry, I didn't—"

"I know you didn't. It's just that I hate being incapacitated in any way. It makes me act like an old bear with a sore paw."

"Well, old bear, I have a remedy for that."

A light jumped into his eyes. "And what might that be?"

"Not what you're thinking, that's for sure."

His face fell. "Damn."

"Don't you ever get enough?"

"Of you? No. I'm hungry right now."

Tiffany flushed, feeling her own insides heat up. Ignoring that, she twisted around, then plucked a peach off the tree. "Here, try this."

He groaned. "Eating a peach wasn't exactly what I had in mind." His voice was low and seductive, even as he took the fruit from her.

Tiffany swallowed around that building heat and watched as he bit into the peach's juicy flesh, never taking his eyes off her.

"How is it?" she asked in a husky tone.

"Fair."

She arched an eyebrow. "You're impossible."

"You're delicious."

Her breathing turned labored. "Not as delicious as that peach."

"Wanna bet?" His voice was thick.

"Let me taste."

"Be my guest." He held the fruit out to her. She felt his burning gaze on her as she sank her teeth into it.

"You're messy," he said, his tone strangled.

Before she could respond, he leaned over and licked the juice off the side of her mouth, then her chin.

"Oh, Garth," she whispered, her knees weakening under his tongue's gentle assault.

"Oh, Garth, what?"

"You know what," she said, pushing him away.

He looked crushed. "Now why'd you go and do that?"

"Because you've had enough, and I have to go." She took his arm and guided the peach back to his mouth. "Munch on that for a while."

"I'll get even with you. And that's a promise."

As she headed toward her car, she didn't bother to turn around. Instead, she just smiled.

"Am I going to live, Doctor?"

"I hope you meant that as a joke."

Garth stared at Dr. Peter Wheeler, then gestured impatiently. "You never know, especially with a ticker like mine."

Even when he walked through the door of the doctor's office, Garth had been tempted to turn around and head back out the door. But he hadn't. He should already have gone in for a checkup, having promised Dr. Landry in Houston that he would.

"As long as you don't do anything stupid, you'll be just fine."

Garth gave the tall, gangly man with the overabundance of white hair and the compassionate green eyes a sharp look. "And what is something stupid?"

"Oh, running ten miles uphill."

Garth harrumphed. "Only an idiot would do anything like that."

Dr. Wheeler smiled. "Then there are lots of idiots around, me included."

"Sorry," Garth said. "It's just that I spend—spent, that is—all my time indoors. I guess I didn't realize there was a world beyond my office."

"Well, now you do, so take advantage of it. Do what you feel like doing. But all the same, don't take anything to the extreme—your work or your play."

"I dreaded coming here."

"I don't see why. You're actually in great shape."

"Until the big one hits, at which time I'll either buy it or become a prime candidate for a transplant."

"That's right, and you could walk out the door today and get run over by a car, too."

"You've made your point, Doctor."

"Good. So go live your life to the fullest. You can't worry about tomorrow."

"I'm afraid that's a hard habit to break. You see, my job requires me to think in terms of tomorrow."

"Well, I suggest you find yourself another job," Dr. Wheeler said flatly.

Garth scratched his head. "Mmm...now that's food for thought, Doc. *Real* food for thought."

That conversation had taken place a while ago. Not long after he watched Tiffany walk out of the orchard, he'd jumped into his truck and driven to Hurricane to see Dr. Wheeler.

Now, back at the cabin, Garth stood at the window, mulling over his options. He'd just hung up from talking to his folks on the phone. When he told them he was considering staying here at least six or seven months out of the year, they'd been stunned yet supportive. He had opted *not* to call Max, for fear he'd have a conniption fit.

Max was deeply challenged by and involved with the pending foreign deal. Garth realized he didn't give a damn about the deal himself.

Right now all he cared about was getting a few cattle, harvesting his peach crop and making love to Tiffany.

Suddenly an unnerving thought struck him, and he felt an unpleasant sensation in his gut. He held her responsible for the changes in him, in his life, yet she wanted no part of that life.

Maybe he should tell her the truth, tell her who he really was. Would that keep her here, knowing that he had money, that he could provide her with all the material things she wanted?

Sweat suddenly rolled off him. Damn, had he lost his mind? What he felt for Tiffany wasn't the real thing. Hell, he didn't know if he would recognize true love even if it slapped him in the face. She was just a good lay. Once she left, he would get over her.

He stared at the peach orchard, only to remember how her taste had mingled with that of the peach. He muttered a few choice words before turning away, his face bleak.

As the old saying went, he had jumped out of the frying pan straight into the fire.

"What do you think?"

"I think you're a miracle worker."

"I'll settle for that."

Garth tweaked her on the nose, then said, for her ears only, "I'll *show* you what I think later, when you get back."

Tiffany's breathing turned ragged. "I'll take you up on that."

"I'm counting on it," he said, his eyes pinning hers.

Tiffany cleared her throat. "Meanwhile, Mr. Dixon, I—*we*—have work to do. I have a truckload of peaches waiting to go to town."

"That you do."

They fell silent for a moment and stared at the orchard, which was virtually bare. For two days now Tiffany, Garth and several farmhands had been picking the fruit and boxing it.

Throughout the backbreaking work, she had kept a close eye on Garth, but he seemed to be just fine. Only once had he caught her staring at him.

"Hey, stop worrying about me, okay? I'm not going to do anything foolish."

"I know, because I'm not going to let you."

"Bossy."

She had laughed, then kept on picking.

Now a truckload was ready to go to Irma's store, where a produce truck from Vegas would be waiting. Garth's crop, along with those from several of his neighbors, had been sold to one of the casino restaurants, thanks to Irma and her connections.

Tiffany had insisted on taking the load into town while Garth remained with the field hands, supervising the cleanup.

"You sure you're up to driving the truck?" he asked, standing beside the door.

The window was down, and she met his concerned gaze head-on. "No problem. I'll be back shortly."

"Be careful."

They stared at each other for a moment. Tiffany was certain he was going to kiss her. When he didn't, she felt a twinge of disappointment. In fact, since they shared that peach in the orchard, he'd been rather standoffish.

Maybe his interest in her was waning.

Halfway into town, she was still grieving over that possibility. She guessed that was why she didn't see the horse until it was too late.

"Oh, no!" she cried, looking on helplessly as the animal darted in front of her.

She slammed on the brakes and veered. It was then that she realized she no longer had control of the vehicle. She saw the ditch, knew she was going to hit it, but there wasn't anything she could do.

She screamed as the truck bucked, then rolled over onto its side.

Fifteen

Tiffany opened her eyes and blinked. She was filled with a surge of relief. She was in her room at the ranch, no longer in the hospital. Breathing a sigh born of that relief, she sat up in bed, tossed the covers back and padded to the window. Once there, she stretched, only to mouth an "Ouch."

Every bone and nerve in her body seemed to squeal. But she ignored that, thankful to have spent only a few hours in the emergency room before being released.

She restretched her muscles; this time the pain was not quite as bad. She just wished her troubled mind would heal as quickly. No such luck. During the majority of the night, her mind had flashed back to the incident, reliving the horror over and over again, just as she had every night since it happened.

Even though her reflexes had kicked in and she had done everything she'd known about, nothing had

worked. For some unknown reason it seemed that she'd
been destined to have that wreck. However, that reason-
ing didn't make her feel one bit better. In fact, she felt
like hell, her thoughts sticking on the certainty that the
peaches would have borne the brunt of her inability to
maintain better control of the truck.

The peaches. Ruined. All of them. Another moan
slipped past her lips. What hadn't flown to kingdom
come and back had been squashed to nothing but a pulp.
Tiffany moaned, not in physical agony this time, but
mental. Such a waste, and she felt totally responsible,
despite the fact that Garth had stressed that he didn't
blame her.

Garth. Her heart upped its pace. She never would forget the panicked look on his face when she had opened
her eyes and found him holding her, frantically calling
out her name, over and over.

Finally she had managed to acknowledge that she
heard him. By then the ambulance had been there, and
the next thing she knew, she'd been in the emergency
room. Later, after the doctor determined that her injuries
weren't life-threatening, that she'd suffered only minor
bruises and abrasions, along with a slight concussion, he
had let Garth into the room.

He'd had a scowl on his face from having been told
to leave while the examination took place. That scowl
hadn't disappeared when he asked, "What the hell happened?"

His sharp words pierced straight through her. "Don't
you dare shout at me!"

"I'm not shouting at you."

"Yes, you are. You're mad."

"If I am, it's only because you scared the living hell
out of me."

"That's not it. You're mad about the peaches."

"That's bull! When you didn't return, I got worried and went looking for you."

She wished she could believe him, but she couldn't, not when he was standing in front of her with his face looking as if it had been carved out of granite. She held herself rigid for fear she would cry.

"What happened?" His voice was a raspy whisper.

She passed her tongue over her dry, trembling lips. "A horse came out of nowhere. I swerved to miss him."

Garth cursed, then leaned over and kissed her briefly on those lips. "I'm serious. You nearly scared me into another heart attack. When I got there and found you on the ground, I..." His voice trailed off.

"I'm so sorry." Tiffany's eyes filled with tears as she peered at him. "The peaches. They're—"

"Screw those damn peaches!" His tone now bordered on violence. "The only thing that matters is that you weren't—aren't—seriously hurt."

"How can you say that?" Tiffany wailed, ignoring the reference to her health. "That load represented a nice sum of money. Now it's all gone."

"Forget that, too," he snapped. "That's not important."

"Well, it is to me. And I know it is to you, too, only you won't admit it."

"It damn sure isn't."

"Why?"

"Because you're more important than a truckload of peaches."

Adrenaline flowed in a warm tingle through her veins as their eyes met and the tension of old crackled between them.

"That's nice to hear," she said in a breathless tone,

lowering her head. What did she want from this man? Was this unspoken thing that hung between them love?

"I mean it," he said in a strained growl.

She faced him again, and noticed that the soft fire in his eyes hadn't been extinguished. Swallowing, she said, "I'm glad, but I still feel terrible about it."

He opened his mouth, as if to say something, but then his lips tightened, stretching into a thin line. Something had flickered in his eyes, too, but she hadn't been able to read what lurked there.

At this point she was too tired, too heartsick, to worry about it. Even though she knew she wasn't thinking rationally, she blamed herself for what had happened. Nothing he could say or do would absolve her of that guilt.

"Look," he said into the building silence, "just forget about the damn peaches, okay?"

"Okay," she lied.

"Good. So let's get you to the ranch and into bed." He paused, his eyes turning hot again. "Alone."

"That's too bad," she murmured in a husky voice.

He chuckled, dispelling another tense moment. "Trust me, that's only temporary."

That thought, his concern for her, warmed her heart all the way to the ranch, where they were greeted with another surprise.

Bridget and Jeremiah had come home. Of course, Bridget was beside herself when Tiffany had walked through the door all banged up. Only after Garth assured her over and over that Tiffany was going to be just fine did Bridget settle down.

Now, two days later, Tiffany was indeed rejoicing that she was all right physically. If only she could get herself straight mentally. Those damn crates of smashed peaches continued to haunt her.

The phone rang, and she jumped, having been lost in thought. She knew either Bridget or Jeremiah would answer it. However, on the fifth unanswered ring, she frowned. Where were her friends? Then it dawned on her. Bridget, accompanied by Jeremiah, was taking her morning walk, something the physical therapist insisted that she do.

Thinking it might be Garth, she reached for the receiver, only to feel instantly disappointed.

The caller was Witch Hazel.

"I hate to be a pest," the other woman said, not mincing words, "but I—the company—needs to know what you've decided."

Tiffany sighed inwardly. She'd been afraid of this call for some time. Now it had come, and she had to face it. Yet she still didn't have an answer. "Today? You have to know today?"

"It's not as if I haven't given you plenty of time here." Hazel's voice was anything but conciliatory. In fact, it had a sharp edge.

"You're right, you have. Give me two more days, and I promise, I'll give you my answer."

"Two days and no more."

"Thanks."

After the conversation was terminated, Tiffany turned from the window, where the sun was out in full force. It was going to be another scorcher, she told herself, making her way into the bathroom, where she showered, then dressed, all the while wrestling with what to do about her ex-company's offer.

If only she hadn't met Garth, the decision would be

an easy one. Refusing to step into that quagmire, she walked into the bedroom, where she pulled up short.

Bridget was sitting on the foot of her unmade bed.

Tiffany smiled. "Morning."

"Are you sure you're okay?"

Tiffany's eyebrows shot up. "Is that your way of telling me I look like warmed-over you-know-what?"

"Sort of." Bridget followed her words with a mischievous smile. "Actually, you look more like you've been in a catfight and lost."

Tiffany again feigned hurt, even as she touched the purple and still-prominent goose egg on the side of her temple. Forcing herself not to grimace, she said, "Now did I tell you that, when you were laid up in bed?"

"Well..." Bridget grinned.

"'Course, I didn't, you turkey."

"It's just that Jeremiah and I have been so worried about you."

"Pooh. Mark me off your list and concentrate on yourself. My stupid accident in no way compares with the seriousness of yours. While you've made a remarkable recovery, you still have a ways to go."

And she did. Bridget had a limp and at times had to use her walker. But all in all, she had come a long way. With Jeremiah there for her, doting on her, she would make a full recovery, which meant Tiffany was no longer needed.

Her stomach knotted at the thought.

"You're in pain," Bridget said. "I saw it just now, in your face."

Tiffany outright lied. "What I am is addled."

Bridget's smile turned into a frown. "I can understand that, especially the way you jackknifed into that ditch."

She shuddered. "You were fortunate you weren't killed."

"Believe me, I know how lucky I am."

Bridget cocked her head, the smile back in place. "I don't recall ever seeing you flat on your back in bed."

"And I hope you never will again. Speaking of rear ends, it's great to see yours is finally up to stay."

"You have such a way with words."

Tiffany gave Bridget a cheeky smile. "I do, don't I?"

Tiffany reached for her friend's hand and squeezed it. Then, in a more serious tone, she added, "All kidding aside, it's great to have you home, and well on your way to a full recovery."

"You almost knocked that in the head, my friend." Bridget reclaimed her hand and placed it on her chest. "When you and Garth walked in the door, and I saw you, I almost had a heart attack on top of everything else."

"Sorry about that. It certainly wasn't in the plans for you to find out that way. In fact, you weren't supposed to find out at all. *You* weren't expected to be home. You were supposed to be still in the hospital."

"We wanted to surprise you."

Tiffany smiled wanly. "Well, it seems we both got surprised."

A silence fell between them.

Finally Bridget cleared her throat, then said, "I wish you'd stay."

"Here, or in Utah?" Tiffany quipped, battling a sinking feeling in the pit of her stomach at what she feared was coming next.

"Both, if you'd like."

"No can do."

"Why?"

Tiffany harrumphed, then laughed a not-so-humorous laugh. "You know why. Jeremiah couldn't run around in the buff."

That comment drew a smile from Bridget. "Most of the time he can't anyway. Remember, we have a child in the house."

"Oops, right. Still, my staying is just not an option."

"So get your own place."

"I can't, and you know it."

"What about Garth?"

Tiffany played innocent. "What about him?"

"I can see right through you, Tiffany Russell. There's something going on between you two. In fact, you both have it bad."

"You're only seeing what you want to see."

"Baloney. I see the way he looks at you and you look at him. And even if I discounted that, when he brought you home from the hospital, that guy was in a world of hurt."

"Probably because I demolished his crop."

Bridget threw up her hands. "You're impossible."

"Witch Hazel's still after me."

"That's great, only I don't think that's where your heart is."

Tiffany gave Bridget the time-out sign. "Give me a break, okay? I'll admit I care about Garth, but there's been no commitment, and I suspect there won't be."

Apparently her tone brooked no argument, because Bridget gave none. Instead, she stood, leaned over and pecked Tiffany on the cheek. "Whatever you do, I'll back you a hundred percent."

"Thanks," Tiffany responded in a watery tone.

"So are you still up for *our* welcome-home party tonight?"

Grateful for the change in subject matter, Tiffany smiled, then nodded. Irma had insisted on the small celebration, which would be fun, Tiffany knew, especially as she would get to see Garth. Her heart raced at the thought. It seemed like aeons since he'd held her....

"Hey, I'm talking to you."

Tiffany flushed. "Sorry, my mind was wandering."

"I just bet it was. And I bet I can guess toward whom."

"Don't start."

Bridget stood. "I wouldn't dream of saying another word."

"I wish that were true."

"You're more beautiful every time I see you."

Tiffany peered down at Garth. "Really?"

"Really, especially when you're on top and I have one of your lovely breasts in each hand."

Feeling her already flushed face turn warmer, Tiffany slid her hand into his chest hair and yanked.

He yelped. "Why'd you do that?"

"Trying to teach you not to talk dirty."

This time he chuckled. "You love it, and you know it."

He was right, she did. Even though they had just made love, she could feel him hardening again inside her. She began to move ever so slowly, even as she said, "Don't you feel any remorse at ducking out on the party early?"

"No," he said thickly, placing his hands on her hips, increasing her pace.

She didn't feel bad, either, though she could imagine what the others had thought, after dinner, when they left and didn't come back. But then, she was among friends.

The only thing was, she hated to see the smug look that was sure to be on Bridget's face.

Right now, though, she had something more important to think about than that. Garth was rock-hard now, and she was about to climax again.

"Let it go, baby," he whispered, rising just enough to surround a nipple with his mouth.

"Ohh," she cried, feeling her wetness soak up his seed.

Later, wrapped in one another's arms, they were almost too exhausted to talk. Ever since they absconded from the party, they had once again thrown caution to the wind and made love over and over, with an almost desperate edge to their lovemaking.

"We should talk," she finally said.

"If you mention those damn peaches again, I'm going to—"

"What?" she whispered, mesmerized by the gleam in his eyes.

"Make love to you again."

Tiffany sucked in her breath, then let it out. "You're insatiable."

"Only with you."

They were quiet for a long moment.

"Back to the peaches," he said at last, "just so you'll have peace of mind. The other two truckloads brought a right nice sum. As far as I'm concerned, I came out ahead."

"Still, if I hadn't—"

"Don't say it again, woman! Forget it. What's important is that you weren't seriously hurt."

She snuggled closer to him. "Thanks."

"I've been thinking."

"About what?"

"What I mentioned a while back—staying here permanently and making a go of the ranch."

She pulled back far enough that she could see his face, the glow of the lamp providing her with that pleasure. "What about your job?"

"If need be, I can do it from here."

"You're serious."

"Damn straight I am. I've found a peace that I never knew existed."

"I'm glad," she muttered, her heart in her throat. Would he by chance ask her to stay here with him? If he did, what would she say?

"So what about you? Now that Bridget is back, what are your plans?"

She thought she heard a vulnerable note, an uncertainty, in his tone, as if he were as unsure about her feelings as she was about his. She wasn't unsure about hers, though. She loved him, and she ached to blurt that out. She didn't, something trapping the words in her throat.

But then, actions always spoke louder than words, anyway. She would prove to him that she loved him. Tomorrow.

"Why don't we talk about that later?" she whispered against his lips.

He groaned and kissed her with renewed passion.

Sixteen

She had to make a decision. Her "tomorrow" was here, and was about to be gone. Tiffany sat on the side of her bed and stared at the telephone. What to do? The same idea that had struck her last night still hugged the edges of her brain.

Gnawing on her bottom lip, she flopped back on the bed and stared at the ceiling. If only she had told Garth that she loved him. Chicken! Berating herself with that ridiculous name somehow made her feel better, though not enough to make her pick up the phone and punch in his number. But then, a woman couldn't declare love for the first time on the phone. It took a setting like the one last evening, when they'd made love.

Would that declaration have changed her dilemma? Had he reciprocated, it certainly would have. If not... She didn't want to think about that, but she had to face reality. If he didn't love her...

Feeling a sudden squeezing inside her chest, Tiffany winced. Push had come to shove. She had to find out Garth's true feelings, then go from there. If lust was all he felt for her, then she would pack her bags and return to Houston, to Hazel and that job offer that was waiting in the wings.

In fact, her thoughts had seesawed between Garth and Hazel all night. Finally, at four this morning, she had gone into the kitchen, having given up on sleep.

Company at that ungodly hour was the last thing she'd expected. That was why she'd been so stunned when she found Bridget sitting at the table, staring out the window into the inky blackness.

"What on earth—"

Bridget smiled. "You, too, huh?"

"If you mean the old sandman wouldn't cooperate, then you're right."

"That's exactly what I meant."

Tiffany poured herself a cup of coffee, then joined Bridget at the table. "You're not sick or anything, are you?"

Bridget's smile strengthened. "No, actually, I just hate to waste too much time sleeping, especially now, after I know how swiftly things can change." She paused, her eyes shadowed. "God, I was so scared, even with Jeremiah sticking to me like glue. Plus, I missed the ranch."

"I still find that amazing."

"Me too."

"Haven't you even started practicing law yet?"

"Sort of. I've got an office in Hurricane, but I've only been to court twice."

"Amazing," Tiffany said again. "I never thought I'd

see the day when you'd be content to cook, can vegetables and look after a child."

Bridget's expression turned dreamy. "It's a miracle, I'll agree. But that's what being in love does to you."

Tiffany felt color stain her cheeks, even as she fell silent under Bridget's close scrutiny.

"Ah, so you *are* in love." It was a statement of fact, rather than a question.

Tiffany's color deepened. "Is it that obvious?"

"Only to me, I'm sure. But then, I know you so well. And when you walked in here, you looked like the cheese had fallen off your cracker into the mud."

If that comment was meant to bring a smile to Tiffany's lips, it worked, though the smile was a fleeting one. "I couldn't have said it better myself."

"Does Garth know?" Bridget asked.

"No, he doesn't."

"I see."

"I wish *I* did." Tiffany massaged her forehead. "I don't think I've ever been so mixed-up."

They fell silent for a while, sipping their coffee.

"So what's the next step?" Bridget finally asked. "You have to make a decision, although you really are welcome to stay here as long as you want."

"I know, but we both know that's not going to happen."

"So are you going to take the witch's offer?"

"Yes, I think so."

"If Garth asked you to stay, would you?"

Tiffany frowned. "I don't know. I love him, no question about that. I realized last night that I've fallen in love for the first time in my life. Still, I don't know if that's enough. I swore I'd never live on a farm again, and now that Garth has decided to stay here indefinitely, maybe forever, then I'd be..." Her voice trailed off.

"Stuck here," Bridget said, finishing the sentence for her.

"Right. And I certainly proved I'm no rancher's wife when I dumped those peaches."

"Don't start on that again. It was an accident, and Garth doesn't hold you responsible. I thought your guilt had been laid to rest."

"I thought so, too, but I can't get the look on his face off my mind. He was devastated by the loss."

"I think you're putting far too much stock in a truck of peaches."

"I don't."

"Well, for the time being, shove that guilt aside and answer one question."

"All right."

"Can you walk away and never see Garth again?"

A pain shot through Tiffany's heart. "No," she said simply.

"Then you have your answer."

"Which is to take a gamble and go for it, huh?"

"Exactly." Bridget's eyes were gentle. "You're enough like me that if you don't, you'll be sorry."

Now, recalling that conversation several hours later, her gaze still focused on the ceiling, Tiffany knew that Bridget had been right. If she refused to take a chance, to gamble on a future with Garth, then she would regret it. She loved him that much.

Yet she had no intention of going to him empty-handed. Bouncing up, she reached for the phone on the bedside table and dialed her banker friend in Houston.

"Tiffany," Wayne Tanner said. "It's great to hear from you."

"Likewise." Before he became her banker, he'd been her friend, having shopped for gifts for his wife in her department. After the first time she waited on him, he'd always requested her.

"So what's up?"

"I want you to do something for me."

"Name it," Wayne said.

A few minutes later Tiffany, with a smile on her face and a spring in her step, headed for Garth's place. After knocking on the door and getting no response, she walked inside.

Didn't he ever answer his door like normal people? She squelched her fear at his failure to respond. "Garth?"

Getting no answer, she walked into the kitchen and peered out the window. She saw him out back, chopping wood. The saliva dried in her mouth as she watched him, bare-chested, swinging the ax down and into the wood.

Watching him was a total aphrodisiac. She squirmed, trying to ignore the wetness that pooled between her thighs, loving him more now than she'd wanted him the night before.

But how did *he* feel about *her?*

Once he received her gift, would she know? Her tongue suddenly cleaved to the roof of her mouth as she turned and started out the back door, only to pause. The kitchen table claimed her attention. Two days' worth of dirty dishes and a pile of papers seemed to glare back at her.

Men! she groaned silently, striding to the table. Should she put things in order, surprise him, before going outside? Yes, she told herself. No way did she intend to stare at him over this mess.

Washing the dishes was the first order; then she concentrated on the table. It was while she was straightening the papers that she paused, an odd feeling coming over her. In her hands were personal documents. Temptation laced with curiosity warred inside her.

Now was her chance to find out more about the man she loved, the man who for the most part had side-stepped her attempts to learn what made him tick. She stared down at envelopes that she knew held bank statements. If she perused those and the other papers, would she perhaps find the final parts of the missing puzzle?

He wouldn't know, she told herself, and she would never tell him, no matter what she learned. She was tempted, so tempted, to take a peek. But if she did, could she live with herself?

She tapped her foot nervously, all the while still clutching the envelopes.

Physically, Garth had never felt better. As usual, though, his mental state was the pits. Now that he had made the decision to remain in Utah, he was as nervous as a whore in church.

But that was not the worst of his problems. While his family had given their full support, his assistant had gone off the deep end.

"You mean to tell me you're *never* coming back?"

Although Garth had expected the question and the attitude, it nonetheless rankled. He felt himself bristle, though he tried to mask his feelings. After all, he'd just dropped a bombshell in Max's ear, one that he wasn't sure he had come to grips with himself.

"I didn't say 'never,' Max."

"Then exactly what *are* you saying?"

"The company's no longer the focus of my life."

Silence.

"Max?"

"What about the Japanese deal?"

"I just got off the phone with them, and as of now, you're in charge."

"Of the entire deal?"

Garth chuckled. "Don't sound so shocked. You're perfectly capable of pulling it off, despite what you think."

"But why? I mean, that deal's what you've wanted, worked night and day on, for years. How can you just..." Max's voice played out.

"Easy," Garth said, his tone smooth and unwavering. "I've found something more important."

"Such as?"

"I'll tell you all about her when I see you."

"*Her!* But—"

"Calm down, before *you* have a heart attack. I'll talk to you later."

Max had still been sputtering when Garth had replaced the receiver.

That conversation had taken place this morning, and since then he'd been outside, riding over the acreage, making mental notes as to what repairs needed to be done. Even though it appeared to be a daunting task, it could be done. Most of the problems stemmed from years of neglect. And money was no object. He had more of that than he could possibly spend.

Once he finished dealing with that, he'd begun chopping up a dead tree for firewood. He paused now to wipe the moisture from his brow, thinking how great his body felt.

He couldn't take credit for the improvement, nor could he cite any medication the doctors had given him. Tiffany was the reason for his miraculous recovery.

Although he hadn't wanted to face it, he had fallen in love with that mouthy blond beauty, something he'd sworn he would never do again. The smile suddenly disappeared as he looked for a shady spot and found it. Leaning against a tree, he mopped his face with a handkerchief.

The problem was that he didn't know how to tell her, and he had no assurance that she felt the same. And even if she did, their goals remained on a collision course. If only he wanted to return to Dallas, to the life-style he'd been forced to leave, then maybe they would have a chance. From day one, she'd made it clear her heart belonged to the city.

Maybe they could compromise. He would be willing. He would be willing to do anything to keep her. Not only did he crave the taste and sight of her body, especially the way she paraded around in those tight-fittin' jeans, but more than that, he was enchanted by her laughter, her feistiness and her sharp mind.

He was addicted, all right, and there was only one cure for that addiction.

Marriage.

He couldn't believe he was thinking such a thing, but he was, which meant he had to tell her the truth about himself.

He cursed. Why the hell had he let her think he was a poor sodbuster to begin with? He knew why. She had goaded him into it, but the ploy now had the potential to explode in his face. No. He wouldn't think like that. He would be positive. Hopefully she would be relieved when he told her that he was a millionaire in disguise. After all, she wanted to marry a man with money.

He didn't know what made him look toward the house. He hadn't heard any noise to indicate he had

company. It didn't matter, especially as his visitor was
Tiffany. Grinning, he moved away from the tree and
made his way toward the back door.

Once inside, he stopped, his gaze settling instantly on
the papers in her hand. His stomach hollowed.

"Just what the hell do you think you're doing?"

Seventeen

Even before she swung around to face him, Garth was sure he would see guilt written on her face. Her body stiffened, which was a dead giveaway. She turned, slowly. To his surprise and chagrin, there were no signs of guilt. Her face was split by a huge grin. As she turned, she laid the papers down.

"Find something funny?"

Although her eyes flashed for a moment, the grin never faded. "I didn't read a word."

Deep furrows creased Garth's forehead as he tried to assess the feelings hammering at him. "Really, now."

"Scout's honor," she said, placing her hand across her chest.

"But?"

"What makes you thinks there's a *but*?" Tiffany's answer and her grin smacked of cheekiness.

A smile unwittingly made its way to his lips, but he

didn't say anything. Instead, he merely gave her a knowing look.

"All right. I was tempted, but I honestly didn't snoop." She paused, and the grin disappeared. "But if I had, would it have been unforgivable? I mean, if you don't have anything to hide—"

Garth thought for a moment, detecting the note of defiance and challenge in her tone. Damn, how had things suddenly gotten so skewed? She was the one who'd gotten caught with her hand in the cookie jar, but she'd managed to turn the tables on him and make him look like the guilty party.

It didn't matter. After all, he'd come to tell her the truth, anyway. He might as well go ahead and get it over with.

"I—"

"I—"

They both broke off suddenly and laughed, tension leaping between them.

Tiffany cleared her throat, then said, "I have something for you."

"You do?" he asked, trying to ignore the sudden tightening in his groin.

"Yeah."

Again that cheeky smile that made him crazy to have her. "You'd best get to the point before I grab you, push you down on the table and have my way with you."

She laughed, then reached into her pocket and pulled out an envelope. She held it out to him.

"For me?" he asked inanely.

Without saying a word, she walked up to him, circled the back of his neck with one hand and pulled his lips down to hers. The kiss was wet, hard and quick. He felt his blood pressure shoot up, but when he would have grabbed her, she pulled away.

"What—?" He heard the agony in his own voice, and he knew she did, too, for she smiled.

"Later."

He groaned as she forced the envelope into his hand, then turned and headed for the door.

"Where are you going?"

She eased around, that sexy light still in her eyes. "To the ranch."

"But—" he sputtered.

She blew him a kiss. "We'll talk after you open your present."

Before he could plead with her to stay and stop his ache, she sauntered out the door.

"Tease," he muttered darkly, sitting down at the table and staring at the sealed envelope. What the hell was going on? Why all the cloak-and-dagger stuff?

Only after he heard her car start did he rip open the flap. A check was enclosed. When he read the amount and the note accompanying it, shock tore through him, shutting off his breath.

Those damn peaches again. She was hell-bent on compensating him for his loss. She was one hardheaded woman. The last thing he needed was her money. Of course, she didn't know that.

He let go of a deep sigh. He couldn't keep her money. He wasn't about to cash it. How he was going to return it without hurting her feelings was another matter altogether. He stared at the name of the bank in Houston. Luckily he knew the president.

Concern and curiosity made Garth reach for the phone. Fifteen minutes later he replaced the receiver, more shock waves running through him.

"Well, I'll be damned," he muttered.

Although he had to use his clout to get the information, he'd found out what he needed to know. The money to cover the check had come from Tiffany's savings, and it had left a considerable dent in her account.

If nothing else, it proved one thing: She was no gold digger. More than that, her unselfish gesture proved she loved him; money *wasn't* all that mattered to her.

Galvanized into action, he lunged to his feet. He would take the plunge. He would ask her to marry him. Now! But what about a ring?

Hell, that would have to come later. Flowers? What about them? Didn't a man who was about to propose to a stubborn woman need that kind of ammunition?

Roses. That was the answer. His mouth was dry even as he picked up the phone and punched in a familiar number.

"Irma, I need your help. How soon can you get me two dozen long-stemmed red roses?"

Whew!

That had been a close call, Tiffany told herself as she parked the car in the drive at the ranch. She didn't get out for a moment, however, using the time to regroup. Her jaw ached from nervous clenching.

Why hadn't he gone ballistic? In his place, she certainly would have. Although she hadn't taken so much as a peek, it would have been hard for her to believe him if the shoe was on the other foot. For some reason, though, he seemed to have taken her meddling extremely well.

She wasn't taking it anywhere near as well. After the fact, she was appalled at her actions. She slammed her hand against her forehead, as if to pound some sense into her head.

Talk about digging up more snakes than she could kill—well, she'd just about done that. She felt she had come about as close to losing him as she possibly could. What had possessed her to think she might get away with such a dishonest thing?

Apparently this time her innocence had been reflected in her face, and Garth had believed her, which was great. She wished now that she'd stayed around when he opened the envelope. At the time she had wanted him to be alone, to think about what her goodwill gesture really meant. Between the lines, the check said, "I love you."

Would he pick up on that? Was he that intuitive? She prayed so. Her future happiness rested on it. Finally getting out of the car, she walked inside.

Bridget was in the living room, the phone in one hand. She covered the receiver and said, "Just in time. It's for you."

Tiffany's lungs suddenly seemed unwilling to do their job. "Is it Garth?"

"No," Bridget said, keeping her hand over the mouthpiece. "I don't recognize this voice at all." She paused. "Just so you'll know, Jeremiah, Taylor and I are all going into Vegas. I have a doctor's appointment."

"I'll see you guys later, then," Tiffany said, reaching for the receiver. Following a tentative hello, she eased down into the nearest chair.

"Tiffany, it's Wayne. Wayne Tanner."

"Is there a problem with the transfer?" she asked, in her usual direct fashion.

"No, none whatsoever."

"Then what's up?"

"It's not what, but who."

"I don't understand."

"I just got off the phone with Garth Dixon."

At first she was too flabbergasted to say anything. At last she found her voice. "How did that happen?"

"He called."

"Do you know him?"

"Know him? Are you serious?"

"Will you just get to the point, Wayne?"

He answered with a question of his own. "Why didn't you tell me why you wanted the money—or rather, who you wanted it for?"

"I didn't think it was necessary." And I still don't, she added silently.

"But why *him*, for crying out loud?"

"Wayne, my patience is wearing thin."

"Don't you know who he is?"

"Suppose you tell me?" Tiffany said, her tone filled with frigid sarcasm.

"Hell, girl, Garth Dixon's up there with the Rockefellers and the Duponts."

"What?"

"That's right. He could buy this bank in a heartbeat—in fact, rumor has it he's considering doing just that."

"You mean—"

"He's loaded, and not only that, he has more clout than the state senate."

"Stop payment on that check," she said, her jaw clenched.

"That's not necessary. He's returning it." Wayne paused. "You want to tell me what's going on?"

"No, I don't. But thanks for calling. I owe you one."

She hung up, but that was as far as she could go. Her

stomach was heaving so badly that she thought she might upchuck. She'd been had.

That low-down worm! That toad! That *liar!* No wonder he'd been so coy, so secretive, about who he was. He hadn't wanted her to know his business. All along he'd been afraid she was only after his money. What a low opinion he must have of her. And to think she loved him. Tears blinded her.

Well, he wouldn't get away with this. No way in hell!

This time, when she reached the cabin, she didn't bother to knock. She simply opened the door and marched inside. He was standing in the middle of the room. Next to him, on the crude desk, sat a huge vase of red roses. He whipped around, and his eyes lit up. "You saved me a trip. I was about to—"

"What? Tell me who you are?"

No way could he have missed the quivering anger in her voice. His eyes narrowed, and the smile fled his lips. "As a matter of fact, that's exactly what I was about to do."

"Oh, really? Why now? Was it in the game plan all along to wait until I made a fool out of myself?" She wouldn't cry; she *wouldn't.* Yet she was perilously close.

His features softened. "That's ridiculous, and you know it."

"I don't know any such thing!"

"Look, I was just about to head over to your place to explain."

Tiffany backed up. "That won't be necessary. Your buddy, my banker, has already done that for you."

Garth's features twisted. "Dammit, Tanner had no right to open his big mouth."

"Is that all you have to say?" she demanded in a shrill voice.

"No. I'm sorry and will you marry me?"

Tiffany shook her head and laughed without mirth. "After this fiasco? You can't be serious? How could I ever trust you, when you didn't trust me?"

"Okay, so I screwed up. I admit that. But—"

"No! Stop right there." The tears were close. She had to get out of there. "To think I was stupid enough to practically empty my savings account, thinking you needed it. God!"

"Don't, Tiffany," he said in a broken voice, edging toward her. "Give me a chance to make it up to you."

She ignored the anguish in his voice. "Forget it. It's too late. You can take your money and go to hell!"

Eighteen

"I can't stand this."

"Me either," Tiffany said, "so please stop whining. You're making it that much harder."

Bridget brushed tears from her eyes, then made a face. "But I don't want you to go." This time her words came out in a wail.

"I don't want to go, either, but I have to."

They were silent for a long moment, during which Tiffany continued to toss her clothing and other articles into her bags. She avoided looking at her friend, for fear she, too, would start bawling.

A week had gone by since that final fiasco with Garth. She had functioned like a robot while hoping he would call or, better yet, come to the ranch and try to make amends. He hadn't, and she knew he wouldn't. Her life was shattered, and there wasn't a damn thing she could do about it.

How had she let it happen? She'd asked herself that question a million times, but she still didn't have an answer. She'd had no intention of opening the door to her heart and letting a man walk in. She almost smiled. Walk in, hell. Garth had stampeded in and camped. Damn him. Damn *her* for letting it happen. She had no one to blame but herself for the mess she was in. How could she stop loving him? How could she stop the horrific pain digging into her soul?

She stifled a moan and, still without speaking, turned her back on Bridget, who was quietly sobbing, and walked to the window. The sun was a golden ball beaming over the mountains. But she hardly noticed its beauty, her mind swirling with another uncertainty she didn't quite know how to handle.

She had missed a period, something she never did, which could mean one of only two things: Either nerves had played havoc with her body, or she was pregnant.

The latter thought sent a dart of panic through her.

"You're holding something back, aren't you?"

Tiffany swung around, thinking again how uncanny it was that Bridget could read her mind. But then, she could read Bridget's, as well. They were not only friends, but true soul mates.

"Yes," Tiffany said simply.

"So tell me."

"I'm trying."

"You've missed a period." Bridget didn't bother to put a question mark at the end of her sentence.

"Yep."

"Which is something you just don't do."

"Bingo."

"Do you feel pregnant?"

In spite of herself, Tiffany smiled. "Now, how would I know that?"

Bridget shrugged. "Beats me. But those who've been there say there are definite signs."

"I'm hoping it's just nerves," Tiffany said, a desperation she couldn't hide in her voice.

"If not..."

"I don't know."

"You mean you'd consider not telling him?"

"He...would have a right to know," Tiffany said in a wobbly voice. "Only—" She couldn't go on.

"I don't think he meant to play you for a fool, Tiff."

"Well, he did, and though I still love him, I can't forgive him. Figure that."

Bridget sighed. "You can tell me to shut up, go to hell or whatever, but I think you're being too pigheaded for your own good. So he kept a secret. Maybe he was scared spitless himself. After all, he's been burned by a woman who married him only for his money. And if I remember correctly, I've heard you spout off numerous times about how it's just as easy to love a man with money as it is one without it." She paused. "Maybe he was just protecting his own backside."

"Maybe, but if you love someone, you don't deliberately deceive them." Only he hadn't ever told her that he loved her, she thought with a pang.

"Okay, hardhead, what are your plans?"

"Back to the old grind, I guess. Witch Hazel came through, and is holding the job."

"And if you *are* pregnant?"

"When the time comes, then I'll just have to deal with it."

Bridget got off the bed, a new onslaught of tears

streaming down her face. "There's nothing I can say or do that'll make you change your mind about leaving?"

"Not unless there's a miracle in the offing."

Bridget smiled. "Who knows? Maybe there will be. Anyway, we can pray for one."

Tiffany didn't respond. Instead, she grabbed her bags and followed Bridget out of the room.

Life sucked. Big-time.

"Isn't that right, boy?"

The horse raised its head, stared at him with those big eyes, then whinnied.

"I knew you'd understand."

Garth removed his Stetson and plopped it on a bent knee. He conceded he had reached an all-time low, having stooped to conversing with his horse.

He laughed a bitter laugh, then wiped his forehead on his arm. He'd been mending fences for several hours now, and he was exhausted. That was the only thing he hadn't been able to overcome—his inability to work long hours nonstop, though the doctor had assured him that his strength would return in due time, as long as he kept stress to a minimum, which was a joke.

Since Tiffany dumped him, he'd already had several bouts of intense pain. God, how he missed her. Even though it hadn't been that long since she told him to go to hell and take his money with him, his heart had experienced a new kind of pain, much worse than before.

Now that the Davises were back, he didn't have an excuse to go to their ranch anymore, so he hadn't seen her. Still, he knew she hadn't left; he'd made it a point to find that out. He'd driven by the ranch last night, and her car hadn't moved from its usual spot.

However, he knew that wouldn't be the case for much

longer. She would be heading out of there ASAP; he figured she'd accepted that job back in Houston.

Dammit, there had to be a way to stop her, to make amends for his lack of trust, for his betrayal. But as yet he hadn't figured out a way, except just to get down on his knees and beg for forgiveness. He grimaced at that thought, only to suddenly rise to his feet.

Why the hell not? If that was what it took to get her back in his life, in his arms, in his bed, then he would do it.

Now!

Five minutes later, he whipped into the Davises' drive. Just as he had feared, Tiffany was about to leave Utah, and *him*, forever. If he'd been a few minutes later, she would have been gone. With that thought in mind, he brought his truck to a halt directly in front of her rental car.

They all turned and stared at him. He remained behind the wheel and watched as Tiffany pulled out of Bridget's arms and opened her car door. Still, her gaze never wavered from him. He saw her shock mirrored in those expressive eyes.

Garth bounded out of the truck and, ignoring the Davises, strode up to Tiffany. "It's your call. If I have to beg, I will."

"Garth—"

"I mean it, Tiffany. I'm not going to let you walk out of my life because of money, you hear?"

Her eyelashes fluttered, while a flush stained her face. Using her apparent confusion to his advantage, he drew her into his arms. Thank God she didn't resist.

"It's not that simple," she whispered, her breath caressing his lips.

"Wrong. It *is* that simple. First, because I love you,

and second, because I don't give a damn about money. If it'll get you back, I'll donate every damn cent I have to charity.''

"You'd do that for me?"

He heard the awe in her voice and saw the light in her eyes, and the icy fear around his heart melted completely. "You're damn right."

"Oh, Garth," she cried, tears beginning to trickle down her cheeks. "I do love you."

"Is that a yes?"

"To what?"

"To marrying me."

She caught her breath. "When?"

"Right now, if that's all right with you."

Jeremiah whistled. Taylor giggled. Bridget hollered, "Let's do it!"

Laughing, Garth suddenly swung Tiffany into his arms and headed toward his truck. "In approximately one hour, you'll be Mrs. Garth Dixon." He paused, his mouth hovering over hers. "Is that what you want?"

She kissed him. "More than I've ever wanted anything."

Epilogue

"Mmm..."

"You like that, huh?"

"I *love* that."

Garth chuckled as he once again dipped his tongue into her navel, one hand lying gently on her distended belly.

She dug her fingers into his shoulders just as the baby kicked. He lifted his head, and the light that sprang into his eyes was a sight she would treasure always.

"Rowdy little devil, isn't he?" Garth's tone was thick.

"Takes after his daddy."

Garth replaced his tongue with his finger, circling her entire stomach, then stopping at the apex of her thighs, where he exerted a slight pressure.

She sucked in her breath as their eyes met and held. "I love you."

"And I love you. And our baby."

Their baby. Those words still had a magic ring to them, as did the words *Mrs. Dixon*. Although they had been married for months now, she had to pinch herself from time to time to make sure she wasn't dreaming.

But then, their wedding had been something dreams were made of. They'd gone straight to Vegas, the Davis family in tow, and gotten married in the same chapel and by the same preacher as Bridget and Jeremiah.

Later, back at Garth's cabin, after making love, hot and heavy, Tiffany had told him that she thought she was pregnant. She'd been right, and he'd been delighted. With each passing day that delight had grown, despite the fact that she'd been sick for much of the time.

Now, well into her pregnancy, she was feeling great. Just last week, in fact, she'd had an ultrasound, learning that the baby was a boy.

"Heck, I was hoping for a girl," Garth had said. "A girl who would look just like you."

"Too bad," she'd responded. "We have to take what we get."

"You mean we can't take it back to the store?"

Later, when she thought about that comment, she'd smiled, just as she was doing now.

"What's so funny?"

"You."

"I'm glad you think so," he said against her lips. Then, following a resounding kiss, he pulled back and said, "You're still thinking, aren't you?"

"About what?" Her tone was innocent.

He snorted. "You know what."

"I haven't made up my mind yet."

And she hadn't. Garth had been after her to check into opening her own women's clothing shop in Vegas.

After they married, however, her mind had been occupied elsewhere. First they'd had to make plans for the baby. Then they'd worked on plans for a new home on a site not far from the cabin.

The only time she had thought about her career was when she flew to Houston to bring closure to things there.

Garth had done the same thing, having made two trips to Dallas to move his business here on a part-time basis and to bring his parents back to meet her. They all seemed to have hit it off well, for which she was thankful. It was nice to be part of a family again.

Now that their house was well on its way to being finished, Garth was insistent that she not give up her dream of owning her own clothing store.

"We can get a live-in nanny to care for the baby," he pressed.

"Is that what you want?"

"I want what you want," he said.

"Okay, then stop mentioning work."

He seemed taken aback, and she grinned, running her hands over his chest. "Right now, I don't want a career. Maybe later, after the baby comes and it's older."

"This decision wouldn't by chance have anything to do with the fact that Bridget's also pregnant?"

"Yes and no, but it's been fun to have been pregnant at the same time. I still can't believe it happened."

"Me either, though I'm glad. Jeremiah's as disgustingly silly as I am, and that's pretty damn silly."

"So I've noticed," Tiffany said teasingly, then added in a sober tone, "but it's more than Bridget. It's about me wanting to care for him myself, to nurse him. That's something I really want to do."

Garth's eyes darkened, then he smiled. "He'll be a lucky fellow."

"Shame on you. As if you don't get your share of me already."

"Now that you've mentioned it, I'm hungry again."

"You can't be."

"Wanna bet?" Garth countered, lowering his head, only to have her stomach lurch again.

Tiffany smiled.

He kissed the spot, then looked back up at her. "Thank you," he whispered.

Love shone from her eyes. "You're welcome, my love."

*   *   *   *   *

Silhouette's newest series

YOURS TRULY

Love when you least expect it.

Where the written word plays a vital role in uniting couples—you're guaranteed a fun and exciting read every time!

Look for Marie Ferrarella's upcoming Yours Truly, *Traci on the Spot*, in March 1997.

Here's a special sneak preview....

1

Morgan Brigham slowly set down his coffee cup on the kitchen table and stared at the comic strip in the center of his paper. It was nestled in among approximately twenty others that were spread out across two pages. But this was the only one he made a point of reading faithfully each morning at breakfast.

This was the only one that mirrored *her* life.

He read each panel twice, as if he couldn't trust his own eyes. But he could. It was there, in black and white.

Morgan folded the paper slowly, thoughtfully, his mind not on his task. So Traci was getting engaged.

The realization gnawed at the lining of his stomach. He hadn't a clue as to why.

He had even less of a clue why he did what he did next.

Abandoning his coffee, now cool, and the newspaper, and ignoring the fact that this was going to make him late for the office, Morgan went to get a sheet of stationery from the den.

He didn't have much time.

Traci Richardson stared at the last frame she had just drawn. Debating, she glanced at the creature sprawled out on the kitchen floor.

"What do you think, Jeremiah? Too blunt?"

The dog, part bloodhound, part mutt, idly looked up from his rawhide bone at the sound of his name. Jeremiah gave her a look she felt free to interpret as ambivalent.

"Fine help you are. What if Daniel actually reads this and puts two and two together?"

Not that there was all that much chance that the man who had proposed to her, the very prosperous and busy Dr. Daniel Thane, would actually see the comic strip she drew for a living. Not unless the strip was taped to a bicuspid he was examining. Lately Daniel had gotten so busy he'd stopped reading anything but the morning headlines of the *Times*.

Still, you never knew. "I don't want to hurt his feelings," Traci continued, using Jeremiah as a sounding board. "It's just that Traci is overwhelmed by Donald's proposal and, see, she thinks the ring is going to swallow her up." To prove her point, Traci held up the drawing for the dog to view.

This time, he didn't even bother to lift his head.

Traci stared moodily at the small velvet box on the kitchen counter. It had sat there since Daniel had asked her to marry him last Sunday. Even if Daniel never read her comic strip, he was going to suspect something eventually. The very fact that she hadn't grabbed the ring from his hand and slid it onto her finger should have told him that she had doubts about their union.

Traci sighed. Daniel was a catch by any definition. So what was her problem? She kept waiting to be struck by that sunny ray of happiness. Daniel said he wanted to take care of her, to fulfill her every wish. And he was even willing to let her think about it before she gave him her answer.

Guilt nibbled at her. She should be dancing up and down, not wavering like a weather vane in a gale.

Pronouncing the strip completed, she scribbled her signature in the corner of the last frame and then sighed. Another week's work put to bed. She glanced at the pile of mail on the counter. She'd been bringing it in steadily from the mailbox since Monday, but the stack had gotten no farther than her kitchen. Sorting letters seemed the least heinous of all the annoying chores that faced her.

Traci paused as she noted a long envelope. Morgan Brigham. Why would Morgan be writing to her?

Curious, she tore open the envelope and quickly scanned the short note inside.

Dear Traci,

I'm putting the summerhouse up for sale. Thought you might want to come up and see it one more time before it goes up on the block. Or make a bid for it yourself. If memory serves, you once said you wanted to buy it. Either way, let me know. My number's on the card.

Take care,
Morgan

P.S. Got a kick out of *Traci on the Spot* this week.

Traci folded the letter. He read her strip. She hadn't known that. A feeling of pride silently coaxed a smile to her lips. After a beat, though, the rest of his note seeped into her consciousness. He was selling the house.

The summerhouse. A faded white building with brick trim. Suddenly, memories flooded her mind. Long, lazy afternoons that felt as if they would never end.

Morgan.

She looked at the far wall in the family room. There was a large framed photograph of her and Morgan standing before the summerhouse. Traci and Morgan. Morgan and Traci. Back then, it seemed their lives had been permanently intertwined. A bittersweet feeling of loss passed over her.

Traci quickly pulled the telephone over to her on the counter and tapped out the number on the keypad.

*   *   *   *   *

Look for TRACI ON THE SPOT
by Marie Ferrarella, coming to
Silhouette YOURS TRULY
in March 1997.

Take 4 bestselling love stories FREE

Plus get a FREE surprise gift!

Special Limited-time Offer

Mail to Silhouette Reader Service™

P.O. Box 609
Fort Erie, Ontario
L2A 5X3

YES! Please send me 4 free Silhouette Desire® novels and my free surprise gift. Then send me 6 brand-new novels every month, which I will receive months before they appear in bookstores. Bill me at the low price of $3.24 each plus 25¢ delivery and GST*. That's the complete price and a savings of over 10% off the cover prices—quite a bargain! I understand that accepting the books and gift places me under no obligation ever to buy any books. I can always return a shipment and cancel at any time. Even if I never buy another book from Silhouette, the 4 free books and the surprise gift are mine to keep forever.

326 BPA A3UY

Name	(PLEASE PRINT)
Address	Apt. No.
City	Province	Postal Code

As seen on TV!
Free Gift Offer

With a Free Gift proof-of-purchase from any Silhouette® book, you can receive a beautiful cubic zirconia pendant.

This gorgeous marquise-shaped stone is a genuine cubic zirconia—accented by an 18" gold tone necklace.

(Approximate retail value $19.95)

Send for yours today...
compliments of ▼ *Silhouette*®
™

To receive your free gift, a cubic zirconia pendant, send us one original proof-of-purchase, photocopies not accepted, from the back of any Silhouette Romance™, Silhouette Desire®, Silhouette Special Edition®, Silhouette Intimate Moments® or Silhouette Yours Truly™ title available in February, March and April at your favorite retail outlet, together with the Free Gift Certificate, plus a check or money order for $1.65 U.S./$2.15 CAN. (do not send cash) to cover postage and handling, payable to Silhouette Free Gift Offer. We will send you the specified gift. Allow 6 to 8 weeks for delivery. Offer good until April 30, 1997 or while quantities last. Offer valid in the U.S. and Canada only.

Free Gift Certificate

Name: _____

Address: _____

City: _____ State/Province: _____ Zip/Postal Code: _____

Mail this certificate, one proof-of-purchase and a check or money order for postage and handling to: SILHOUETTE FREE GIFT OFFER 1997. In the U.S.: 3010 Walden Avenue, P.O. Box 9077, Buffalo NY 14269-9077. In Canada: P.O. Box 613, Fort Erie, Ontario L2Z 5X3.

FREE GIFT OFFER
084-KFD

ONE PROOF-OF-PURCHASE

To collect your fabulous FREE GIFT, a cubic zirconia pendant, you must include this original proof-of-purchase for each gift with the properly completed Free Gift Certificate.

084-KFD

SILHOUETTE... Where Passion Lives

Order these Silhouette favorites today!
Now you can receive a discount by ordering two or more titles!

SD#05988	HUSBAND: OPTIONAL by Marie Ferrarella	$3.50 U.S. ☐ /$3.99 CAN. ☐
SD#76028	MIDNIGHT BRIDE by Barbara McCauley	$3.50 U.S. ☐ /$3.99 CAN. ☐
IM#07705	A COWBOY'S HEART by Doreen Roberts	$3.99 U.S. ☐ /$4.50 CAN. ☐
IM#07613	A QUESTION OF JUSTICE by Rachel Lee	$3.50 U.S. ☐ /$3.99 CAN. ☐
SSE#24018	FOR LOVE OF HER CHILD by Tracy Sinclair	$3.99 U.S. ☐ /$4.50CAN. ☐
SSE#24052	DADDY OF THE HOUSE by Diana Whitney	$3.99 U.S. ☐ /$4.50CAN. ☐
SR#19133	MAIL ORDER WIFE by Phyllis Halldorson	$3.25 U.S. ☐ /$3.75 CAN. ☐
SR#19158	DADDY ON THE RUN by Carla Cassidy	$3.25 U.S. ☐ /$3.75 CAN. ☐
YT#52014	HOW MUCH IS THAT COUPLE IN THE WINDOW? by Lori Herter	$3.50 U.S. ☐ /$3.99 CAN. ☐
YT#52015	IT HAPPENED ONE WEEK by JoAnn Ross	$3.50 U.S. ☐ /$3.99 CAN. ☐

(Limited quantities available on certain titles.)

TOTAL AMOUNT	$_____
DEDUCT: 10% DISCOUNT FOR 2+ BOOKS	$_____
POSTAGE & HANDLING ($1.00 for one book, 50¢ for each additional)	$_____
APPLICABLE TAXES*	$_____
TOTAL PAYABLE	$_____

(check or money order—please do not send cash)

To order, complete this form and send it, along with a check or money order for the total above, payable to Silhouette Books, to: **In the U.S.:** 3010 Walden Avenue, P.O. Box 9077, Buffalo, NY 14269-9077; **In Canada:** P.O. Box 636, Fort Erie, Ontario, L2A 5X3.

Name:_____

Address:_____City:_____

State/Prov.:_____ Zip/Postal Code:_____

*New York residents remit applicable sales taxes.
Canadian residents remit applicable GST and provincial taxes.

Silhouette®

SBACK-SN4

You're About to Become a *Privileged Woman*

Reap the rewards of fabulous free gifts and benefits with proofs-of-purchase from Silhouette and Harlequin books

Pages & Privileges™

It's our way of thanking you for buying our books at your favorite retail stores.

Pages & Privileges ™

✂

PROOF OF PURCHASE
SD-PP23
Offer expires March 31, 1997

Harlequin and Silhouette—
the most privileged readers in the world!

For more information about Harlequin and Silhouette's PAGES & PRIVILEGES program call the Pages & Privileges Benefits Desk: 1-503-794-2499

Silhouette®

SD-PP23